DAN WILLADSEN

I0623297

DIG

DEEP

A Novel

———

We Be Wet, Inc.

This is a work of fiction. Names, characters, businesses, places, events, and incidents are either the products of the author's imagination or used in a fictitious manner. Any resemblance to actual persons, living or dead, or actual events is entirely coincidental. The views expressed by the characters do not necessarily reflect those of the author.

ISBN: 979-8-9911561-0-3

Published by We Be Wet, Inc.

Printed in the U.S.A.

First edition, August 2024

To my family.

—

A BRIEF NOTE
FROM THE AUTHOR

While Kyle's escapades found in the pages of this novel are fictitious, the ever-increasing challenges facing today's teachers are very real. To all who continue to educate with patience, kindness, and a sense of humor, thank you for your perseverance; and to all who read this book, thank you for giving me a chance. I hope you enjoy my first novel!

Chapter 1

Kyle Kennedy, to the principal's office, please. Kyle Kennedy, to the principal's office. It was the last day of school. In a few short hours, eighth grade would be a distant memory, but there I was, on my way to the principal's office for the third time in three days. Though I had become rather familiar with the principal's office over the course of the year, this was the first time that I'd been sent there three days in a row.

The first of the three trips was the fault of Sarah Delvey, a big-mouthed tattletale, and Mrs. Kratz, a math teacher with no sense of humor. On Monday, whenever Mrs. Kratz would turn her back to us to write on the board, I'd whisper, "Do it." Then, of course, she'd whip her head around to see who said it or to see what the terrible "it" was that someone was being encouraged to do. It was hilarious.

After the fourth or fifth time, though, she was such a wreck that she just sat down at her desk and glared at us. We became quiet and looked around at each other, unsure of what we should do. Then I noticed that Sarah Delvy, whose desk sat to the right of mine, had her skinny little hand raised. I looked at her and mouthed, "No!" She looked back at me with a malevolent grin and whispered, "You are in so much trouble, and I can't wait to see you kicked out of this school FOR-EV-ER." Of course, Mrs. Kratz called on her, and the next thing I knew, I was on my way to the principal's office.

Chapter 2

The second of the three trips involved a bottle of epoxy pilfered from shop class and the school supplies located on Mr. Hansen's desk. Mr. Hansen was our English teacher, and he had a rule that *nobody* was to come within six feet of his desk. He called the six-foot perimeter "The Safe Zone" and marked it off with blue painter's tape.

So when it came to pass that by the end of class on Tuesday five pens, two pencils, a scissors, and a stapler were all permanently affixed to his desk in the shape of a smiley face, I was certain that it would go down as one of the world's greatest unsolved mysteries.

Unfortunately, Mr. Hansen's powers of observation were quite astute, and it didn't take him long to notice the tape dispenser that I'd accidentally glued to my right hand. And just like that, one of the world's greatest mysteries was solved.

Chapter 3

My final trip to the office came about as a result of what I called *The Ultimate Culminating Activity*. Most teachers on the last day of school would just collect books and let us talk and play games, but not Mrs. Greenbaum. Mrs. Greenbaum was an old-school science teacher who believed that every minute of every class period should be used for learning. As a result, she scheduled a test for the last day of school and called it a *culminating learning assessment*. In any event, who wants to take a test on the last day of school?

Science was first period, so while Mrs. Greenbaum was out in the hall supervising students, I was in the classroom setting the wheels of my plan in motion. First, I had Mike, who always wore boots to school, give them to me and then hide behind the door. Next, I quickly coached up the girls on what to do when Mrs. Greenbaum walked into the room. Finally, I opened the window to our second story classroom, took out the screen, and held both boots outside the window upside down so that the tops were below the windowsill.

When the first period bell rang, several events took place in quick succession: Mrs. Greenbaum walked into the room. The girls screamed, "Kyle, don't drop him!" Mrs. Greenbaum, certain that she was seeing one of her students being dangled out the window by his feet, yelled, "No!" Feigning surprise, I turned, said *"What?"*, and let go of the boots.

As she saw the boots sink out of sight, Mrs. Greenbaum began to take a step forward as though she wanted to somehow come to the rescue of her falling student, but she never made it. When a bootless Mike stepped out from behind the door and said, *"What's up?"*, it was just too much for the poor thing. Her eyes got wide, rolled back into her head, and like an accordion, her body seemed to deflate and cascade into a crumpled, lifeless heap.

I ran to the phone to call the office, but other

teachers had heard the commotion and were already at her side. After moments that seemed like hours, Mrs. Greenbaum began to stir, and we all let out a sigh of relief. Then came the inevitable announcement: "Kyle Kennedy, to the principal's office, please. Kyle Kennedy, to the principal's office."

Chapter 4

Previous trips to the principal's office had been rather uneventful: a stern talking to, scrawling my signature on a piece of paper acknowledging my wrongdoing with a promise to never do it again, and then a warning of harsher consequences for further transgressions. Easy peasy, nice and easy. Since it was the last day of school, and since the adults in our school were most likely as eager to put the school year behind them as we students were, I was confident that my sentence would again be light, and I would soon be on my way.

When I opened the door to the office, however, I got the feeling that things might be different this time. Mrs. Buchman, the principal's secretary, who I had become rather well-acquainted with over the course of the year due to my many trips to the office, didn't seem to appreciate my visit with her normal enthusiasm. "Have a seat, Kyle." No smile. No chit-chat. All business. I was going to point out to her that she should do a better job of creating a welcoming environment, but one look at her stern countenance helped me to decide that at least for the moment, discretion was the better part of valor. I took a seat.

The chairs in the office were not comfortable. They were the type of chairs made for looks and not for sitting: Sticky red vinyl plastered over hard sharp-edged cushions. No armrests. Chair legs too tall for your feet to rest comfortably on the ground. Backs too straight to comfortably recline. As I sat there shifting my bottom from side-to-side searching for a less painful position, I got to thinking that perhaps whoever purchased those chairs wasn't thinking about looks at all. Perhaps those chairs were the product of some diabolical mind plotting to surreptitiously punish anyone unfortunate enough to have to sit in them. Oh well, I thought to myself. It couldn't be too much longer until Mr. Burns called me in – but it was.

I took out my phone. At Oak Grove Junior

High, the use of cell phones was a bit of a gray area. We could use them sometimes, like in the halls, cafeteria, and the rooms of some of our more progressive teachers; however, at other times they were strictly forbidden, like in the rooms of crusty old teachers who expected you to "stay on task" and "practice self-control" – and apparently in the office as well.

Without looking up, and in a tired, flat voice, Mrs. Buchman said, "Kyle, put your phone away."

"Can I just use it for a minute? I need to check something."

"No."

"A second?"

"No. Put it away or give it to me."

I put it away.

Chapter 5

Sitting in the office is generally a snore, but if you sit still and don't draw attention to yourself, the office staff and other visitors tend to not pay attention to you, and if you use your eyes and ears, it can sometimes even be somewhat entertaining or informative. For instance, as I sat there, three students came in needing to see the nurse (two for headaches and one with a bloody nose), two students came in to sign out for orthodontist appointments, and one baseball coach came in with some information that actually pertained to me.

"Mrs. Buchman," said Coach Cavinaugh, "would you please announce during lunch that this year's summer baseball roster is posted in the office? I'd like the players to know who made the team before they leave today."

"I certainly will."

"Thank you," said the coach, as he tacked a piece of paper to the office bulletin board. When he turned to leave, Coach Cavinaugh seemed to make an intentional effort not to make eye contact with me – not a good sign.

I looked at what he had posted. The font on the paper was large, and I have good eyes, so even from several feet away, I could clearly see the list of names. And my name was not on the list. Instead, where my name should have been was another – and it was a name that I didn't recognize: Joey Jefferson. I hadn't really noticed any new kids at try-outs, but evidently the coaches had.

I liked baseball well enough, but baseball really didn't seem to like me. When I was in Little League, I wanted to be a pitcher, but since my dad wasn't one of the many volunteer coaches, that dream didn't last long. On our team, if your dad didn't coach, you didn't pitch – so I got a lot of experience playing all the other positions – at least for a while. Unfortunately, I just didn't enjoy playing those other positions, and I guess it showed. Soon, I found myself watching from the bench more than playing in the field.

Even though I didn't play much, hanging out with the other guys on the team had been fun, so I'd stuck it out throughout elementary school and even 7th grade. (There was a no-cut rule in 7th grade.) Even I, though, could see that my lack of playing time, lack of practice reps, and lack of enthusiasm resulted in the skills of my peers surpassing my own; so not seeing my name on this year's roster really wasn't a surprise, but it still stung a little.

Chapter 6

First period came to an end. The outer wall of the office was made up entirely of glass, so I could clearly see the waves of excited students full of last-day exuberance filling the halls – and they could see me. Since it was only the end of first period, however, word had not yet spread as to why I was there. As a result, I got more than a few questioning looks. In return, I could only shrug and give them my best "Don't-worry-about-me-I've-got-this" smile.

There were a few, though, that had been in my science class or had heard about my escapade, and those students would pass by and give me a thumbs up or a knowing smile, which gave me confidence that my efforts to bring some excitement into our school were appreciated by my fellow students and had not been in vain.

Chapter 7

By the time the end of second period was rolling around, I was beginning to wonder what the hold-up was with Principal Burns. I'd been sitting for well over an hour, and my theory about the office chairs actually being torture devices for wayward students was beginning to gain momentum. Since it was a hot day, I'd worn shorts to school, and the backs of my legs were beginning to sweat and stick to the vinyl seat. Like ripping off adhesive bandages, I'd gently lift one leg and then the other taking turns giving each a little breathing room. Unfortunately, every leg lift was accompanied by a squishy wet ripping sound: Sshhriiiiip... Sshhriiiiip... Sshhriiiip – a sound that soon began to annoy Mrs. Buchman.

"Kyle! Do you have to do that?"

I didn't realize that her question was rhetorical, so I gave her what I thought was a clear, honest, and forthright answer: "Yes."

She glared at me. "Well, if you can't sit there like you're supposed to, then you can just stand. Go over there and stand by the wall."

Feeling confused and unjustly punished, I trudged across the room and stood below a poster which read: *The truth will set you free*.

Sitting had been bad. Standing was worse. I shifted to one side. Then the other. Raised up on my toes. Rocked back and forth. (Which drew the disapproving eye of Mrs. Buchman.) I stood with my feet wide. Then together. When I wasn't sure if I could stand it anymore, the second period bell rang, and students again began parading by, distracting me from my plight. This time, however, I could see that word had spread and that I'd become a bit of a celebrity. Curious looks were mostly replaced with smiles and nods, but strangely enough, there were also some scowls and glares as well. I wondered what that was about? Couldn't they take a joke? Where was their sense of humor? Didn't they appreciate how much planning went into pulling off *The Ultimate Culminating Activity*? Then the halls were empty, and I was still in the office. Standing.

Chapter 8

"Mrs. Buchman, may I use the restroom?" I asked as politely as I was able.

"You don't need to use the bathroom. You're just bored and want to get out of here."

I tried again, this time with more urgency. "Please? I really need to go."

Contemplating her decision, she scrutinized me over the top of her too-big-for-her-face purple eyeglasses. I don't know if Mrs. Buchman was a good judge of all human character, but she was certainly an excellent judge of my own. Playing the bathroom card, however, had her over a barrel. Not finding any other suitable options, she reluctantly gave in. "Okay. You've got three minutes."

Hustling out the door, I found myself in a now

lifeless hallway. I headed towards the restroom, but when I got there, I came to an abrupt stop. At our school, the cooks always helped us celebrate the last day of school by serving us pizza. And even though it was only midmorning, I could already smell the aroma of fresh-baked pizza wafting from the cafeteria. My stomach growled. The cooks' pizza was always good, but I sometimes wondered how much better it'd be fresh out of the oven.

Inspiration strikes at unexpected times and unusual places. That day, it struck at 10:42 outside of the boys' restroom. I did an abrupt 180 and ran back to the office. (Mrs. Buchman was correct. I didn't need to go.) Throwing open the door, I announced to Mrs. Buchman in my most urgent voice, "Mr. Smith says he needs you in the library right away! You're supposed to hurry!" Mr. Smith was our school librarian, and the likelihood of his having an immediate need for Mrs. Buchman's presence was dubious. Mrs. Buchman was a sharp old bird, and I could tell that she didn't want to believe me; however, it didn't take her long to realize that she dare not face the consequences of NOT believing, so she said, "Stay right here. Don't touch ANYTHING."

As I've mentioned before, by the end of my eighth-grade year, I had become quite familiar with the principal's office and had observed its routines and procedures on a fairly regular basis. As a result, it took no time for me to slip behind the counter, flip the switch to the intercom, and announce: "Your attention, please. Your attention, please. This is not a drill. Please exit the building. This is not a drill. Please exit the building."

Students and teachers began flooding the hallways on their way out of the building. I slipped from behind the counter into the hall to join them. However, I had no intention of exiting the building. Like a salmon swimming upstream, I headed to the cafeteria. That is where, fifteen minutes and three slices of pizza later, Mr. Burns found me.

Chapter 9

For the second time in a day, I was headed to the principal's office. This time, though, there would be no waiting. Mr. Burns hauled me into his office and planted me firmly on a hard straight-backed chair directly in front of his desk. Huffing and puffing, he stalked around the room, intermittently giving me looks that made my stomach churn. Perhaps at one time, many years and several hundred school lunches ago, Mr. Burns may have been a handsome man; but now on the other side of sixty, he had kind of gone to seed: big round belly, flabby jowls, and perched on top of his head was a shiny island of baldness floating in a sea of bristly gray hair.

Finally running out of steam, he wedged himself behind his desk. Face red, beads of sweat blanketing his forehead, Mr. Burns glared at me. Sitting across from me was *not* a happy man. Though I tried to look him in the eye, I just couldn't keep my gaze from straying to his left nostril. There, precariously perched on a rogue nose hair, was a brave little booger. With every angry breath, the booger did a little jiggly dance.

I really did try hard not to laugh. I clamped my lips together, dug my toes into the soles of my shoes, and bit the side of my cheek until I tasted blood. But it was all in vain. The sides of my mouth began to twitch, my eyes started to water, and an explosion of laughter erupted from my lips.

Mr. Burns immediately did some erupting of his own. "Do you think this is funny? Stop that laughing!"

I tried to stop. I really did. My belly hurt, and I was struggling to catch my breath. But each time that I thought I was done, I'd catch a glimpse of that jiggling little booger and start all over again. Finally, Mr. Burns yelled, "Stop it!" with such force that the valiant booger lost its hold and was sent flying through the air. Its trajectory unhindered, it made a perfect arc and eventually came to rest amid the tiny flecks of spit that sprinkled the top of his desk like dandruff. Actually, upon closer inspection, some of the flecks appeared to perhaps actually *be* dandruff. This final scene proved too much. I fell from my chair in fits of uncontrollable laughter.

Chapter 10

Eventually, I regained my senses and slid back onto my chair. Mr. Burns seemed to have calmed down somewhat himself. "That's better," he said. "Now we can get to the bottom of this. Tell me, Kyle, just what were you thinking?" I would have thought Mr. Burns, who obviously had been in education since the time of blackboards, would have known better than to ask an eighth-grade boy what he was thinking. When analyzing my motivation for doing something inexplicable, I could only mutter the quintessential answer given by *any* eighth-grade boy subjected to similar circumstances: "I don't know."

"You don't know?! You don't know?! Well, Mister, maybe you will know by the time the police get here."

"The police?"

"Yes, the police. Faking an emergency is considered a crime. I've also contacted your parents. They should be here shortly."

"My parents?"

"Of course. Not only is it important for schools and parents to be on the same page, but you're only fourteen, so they need to be here during questioning."

"Questioning?"

"Kyle, do you have a problem with your hearing?"

"I don't know."

Mr. Burns let out an exasperated sigh. "I'll tell you what we're going to do. You are going to sit there and listen, you are going to answer when spoken to, and you're not going to repeat everything I say. Okay?"

"Okay."

Mr. Burns stood up, walked to the window and gazed out at the parking lot. "Kyle, what is the most important thing that we've tried to teach you at Oak Grove?"

"I don't know."

"Try again."

"Math?"

"Again."

"Science?"

"What do we talk about at every single assembly? What is the first thing addressed in our student handbook? What is a part of every teacher's classroom syllabus? What do I remind students of in the lunchroom almost every single day?"

"To have self-control?"

"Thank you. Self-control." Mr. Burns seemed to see what he had been looking for and turned away from the window. "The most important thing we've tried to teach you here at Oak Grove is self-control. Without self-control, you aren't able to take the time to predict outcomes, and if you can't predict outcomes, you can't make good choices, and if you don't make good choices, *bad things happen.* Mr. Kennedy, what you did today was a bad thing. A very bad thing. And now you will have to face some very bad consequences."

Chapter 11

As it turned out, the bearer of my consequences was a young policeman who didn't look much older than some of the kids in my class. Accompanying him were my parents, who I'm sure were not thrilled about having to get off work to come to my rescue. Introductions were made, chairs were offered, and I felt like I was greatly outnumbered.

Then, in his most serious tone of voice, Mr. Burns got down to business. "Mr. and Mrs. Kennedy, Officer Davidson, Kyle has been involved in several major incidents of misconduct today: jeopardizing the health of a teacher, lying to school personnel, stealing food from the cafeteria, and initiating a fake emergency evacuation." Directing his attention to me, he continued, "Kyle, will you please share with Officer Davidson and your parents what you were thinking when you decided to commit these most egregious acts?"

"Hold on a second," interrupted Officer Davidson. "Kyle, before you say anything, I will need to read you your Miranda rights."

"Is that really necessary?" asked my mom. "He's only fourteen."

"That may be," replied Officer Davidson, "but it also sounds like he may have committed several crimes, and we need to cover all of our bases." Turning to me he said, "You have the right to remain silent. Anything you say can and will be used against you in the court of law. You have the right to an attorney. If you cannot afford an attorney, one will be appointed for you. Kyle, do you understand your rights as I've read them to you?"

"Yes."

"In that case," continued Officer Davidson, "would you please tell us why we are all here."

I looked at my parents, dressed in business casual, taking the occasional peek at their phones, obviously upset with what I did yet anxious to get it over with and back to their more predictable and orderly world of work. I looked at Officer

Davidson: young, eager, hopeful. And I looked at Mr. Burns, who seemed quite calm and professional now that he had an adult audience, but I could still see the remnants of his previous rant sprinkled across his desk.

At that moment, I could have told my expectant audience a lot of things. I could have told them that I wasn't ready for the school year to end. That I would miss the routine, the structure, the safety. That I really enjoyed being around my friends and even my teachers – and especially the attention I got from them when I misbehaved. I could have told them that I was dreading summer vacation. That I hadn't made the baseball team and probably wouldn't be seeing much of my friends until school started next fall. I could have told them that I feared loneliness, going to high school, the future. I could have told them a lot of things. But I didn't. Instead, all I could say was "I don't know."

Chapter 12

Officer Davidson handed me an official looking paper. "This is a summons," he said. "It is not an admission of guilt. It just means that you need to contact the courthouse and set a date to meet with the judge."

"A judge?" I asked. "Why do I have to meet with a judge? I didn't hurt anyone. Not really. I just had a little fun and tried to add some entertainment to a boring day."

Officer Davidson frowned. "You broke the law. When you break the law, you face the consequences. The judge will decide your punishment."

"That's only partially true," corrected Mr. Burns. "The judge will impose a judicial sentence, but Oak

Grove will enforce a punishment as well. Kyle, I am sorry, but you've left me with no other choice but to suspend you until next month's school board meeting, at which time we will discuss your permanent expulsion."

"You mean," squeaked my mom, "Kyle won't be able to attend school here anymore?"

"It's a possibility," stated Mr. Burns.

"Oh, no!" she replied. "All of his friends are here."

My dad, who liked the *idea* of having a son who played ball but seldom cared enough to come to a game, leaned conspiratorially towards Mr. Burns and asked, "What about baseball? He can still play ball even if he is suspended, can't he?"

My ears burned, and my face got red.

"What?" interrupted my mom, noticing my discomfort.

"I didn't make the team," I mumbled.

Now it was my dad's turn to have a red face. "What do you mean you didn't make the team?!" he bellowed. "How could you not make the team?"

My eyes went to the floor. "I don't know."

"Then I guess you have a *really long* summer ahead of you," he said, "because you are grounded until further notice. Under no circumstances will you be allowed to leave the house without our permission."

The meeting ended with my parents giving me "The Disappointed Speech" in front of Mr. Burns and Officer Davidson to show what responsible parents they were and that it wasn't *their* fault that their son was a miscreant. Then there was the obligatory sliding of chairs, shaking of hands, and stuffy adult politeness as the meeting mercifully came to an end.

Leaving the school, my dad said, "Your mom and I need to get back to work. We'll talk more about this when we get home."

"Can one of you give me a ride?" I asked.

"No," said my mom. "You can walk. And while you're walking, maybe you can spend some time contemplating the error of your ways."

Chapter 13

No one is freer than the person who has nothing to lose. So when I got to my house, I didn't go inside. Instead, I went to the garage, grabbed my fishing pole, and kept on walking. In twenty minutes, I was at the lake.

We lived in a resort town. For years, people had been coming to the area to enjoy the lake's sparkling clear waters, endless sand beaches, and excellent fishing. They also came for a considerable amount of man-made entertainment – restaurants, resorts, and a lakeside amusement park.

Summer homes ringed the lake. Larger and much more expensive than any of the houses my friends and I lived in, they symbolized the class chasm between the "summer people" and the "locals". The relationship between the two factions was both symbiotic and fractious: symbiotic in that the locals relied heavily on the money brought in by the summer people, and the summer people relied heavily on the goods and services provided by the locals; fractious in that both parties having what the other couldn't created a certain amount of animosity.

Many locals used to live in small homes or cottages on the lake. As demand for lakeshore property increased, property values increased – as did property taxes. Lakeshore homes that had been handed down from generation to generation were now worth so much money that the locals could no longer afford to pay the taxes required to live there, so they sold their homes to those who could pay: summer people. Even though locals profited well from selling, there were still hard feelings because many of those forced to sell would rather have had their home instead of the money. And summer people, even if they were of the few who lived there year-round, would never be considered locals. Summer people were courted, pandered to, and tolerated – but seldom embraced.

Chapter 14

The place I had chosen to fish was a public access dock at the ancient not-yet-open-for-the-summer amusement park. Memorial Day weekend began the tourist season, and soon it would be too noisy and crowded for fishing there except for early in the morning or late at night – but until then, I had it to myself. Or at least, so I thought. I had just started to make my first cast when a deep gravelly voice from behind me said, "Traveling kind of light today, aren't you? No bait? No tackle box?"

When I turned around, I was confronted by a barrel-chested giant of a man. He was looking at me through intelligent soft blue eyes framed by a thick white beard and bushy eyebrows. Cut-off jeans housed tree trunk legs, and a red flannel shirt with rolled up sleeves revealed bulging biceps and forearms of steel. One enormous pawlike hand held a metal detector, the other a long-handled sand scoop.

"Yeah," I said, looking at the gold bladed spinner dangling at the end of my fishing pole. "It's one of those days where I'm more interested in the fishing than the catching."

"Uh-huh. I've had those kinds of days."

"So do you ever find anything with that?" I said, pointing to his detector.

"Sometimes."

"Like what? Gold jewelry? Silver coins?"

"Actually, the metal I mostly find is aluminum. Aluminum pull tabs!" Then he let out an enormous belly laugh that was so loud and violent that it shook the dock like a herd of elephants crossing a bridge. Red faced and eyes streaming tears, he guffawed and guffawed. His joke wasn't funny, but his laughter was contagious. I soon found myself joining him, laughing until my sides hurt. Trying to catch my breath, I pointed to the detector and wheezed, "Will you show me how to do that?"

"Sure. By the way, my name's Emmet, Emmet Arnold" he said, holding out his hand.

For a brief moment I had a feeling of trepidation. "Stranger danger" was very real, and this man could easily haul me away or break me in two. But then again, I thought to myself, what did I have to lose? I shook Emmet's hand. His giant mitt completely engulfed my own. His grip was firm and friendly, though it also undoubtedly had the capability to crush.

Trying to match his grip, I said, "I'm Kyle Kennedy."

A shadow briefly crossed his face, and with a smile I couldn't quite read, he said, "Pleased to meet you, Kyle Kennedy."

Chapter 15

In a few lumbering strides, Emmet was soon off the dock and onto the sand beach. I followed. "Put these headphones around your neck instead of on your ears," he instructed. "That way, we both can hear the signals." He turned on the detector and there was a momentary beep, then silence. "Hold the coil a couple of inches above the ground and swing it back and forth in an arc."

People with metal detectors were not an uncommon sight at the old amusement park. While fishing, I'd watched them methodically swinging their machines back and forth as they slowly strolled up and down the beach, occasionally stopping to scoop something from the sand. As a result, I was somewhat familiar with what I was supposed to do, but I'd never heard the different beeps the machines made or understood what they were telling the operator.

"There are all sorts of metal detectors," he said, "and they all seem to make their own types of sounds. This one, for instance, makes high-pitched sounds when you swing across a coin or silver ring. Here, swing your coil over this." He dropped a dime onto the sand. As soon as I swung my coil over the coin, a loud high-pitched beep suddenly popped into my ears.

"Hey! I hear it!" I yelled in surprise.

"Of course, you can," he chortled. "Now, if you happen to swing your coil over iron or steel, you'll hear a low-pitched sound, like this." He threw a nail onto the sand, and when I swung the coil over it, I heard a low-pitched bonk.

A light came on in my head. "So if you don't want to dig as much junk, you don't dig the low sounds, right?"

"Right."

He tossed a pull tab onto the sand. "Now, if you happen to run your coil over an aluminum pull tab, you'll hear a medium tone somewhere between the other two tones." I ran my coil over it, and a medium-toned zip met my ears.

"Hey! That's pretty cool!" I said. "What does gold sound like?"

"Unfortunately, the sound of gold almost always sounds exactly like a pull tab."

He had a gold band on his left hand and waved it across the face of the coil.

"You're right! It sounds like a pull tab. So in order to find gold rings, you have to also dig up all those aluminum pull tabs?"

"Exactly. You're a fast learner. Why don't we make our way down the beach and see what we can find? You swing, I'll dig. Make sure to keep your coil close to the ground and overlap each swing so you don't miss anything. Also, if you sort of shuffle your feet as you move along, it's easy to see where you've been when you head back the other way."

Chapter 16

As I began shuffling along swinging the detector, I soon heard a mid-toned zip, and Emmet said, "Swing your coil back and forth in an X so we can pinpoint exactly where your target is."

I did as instructed. With a deft swing of the scoop, Emmet swept up a heaping pile of sand. As it sifted through the holes in the scoop, I waited in anticipation. Soon the sand was gone, and a lonely pull tab was left sitting in the bottom of the scoop.

"Aw, shucks!" I said, but really not the least bit disappointed. I had never found anything with a metal detector before, so finding anything at all, even a pull tab, was exciting.

"Unfortunately," ruminated Emmet, "people are pigs, and you'll find all sorts of pull tabs, pop tops, and other garbage while you're looking for the good stuff. I've started keeping track of the garbage that I find, and last year I removed over twenty-five gallons of litter from beaches."

"So you're kind of doing a public service by cleaning up the beaches, aren't you?"

"I guess you could look at it that way," Emmet said with a laugh, "though that certainly has never been my primary objective!"

"Then what *is* your primary objective?" I asked. "Finding treasure? Getting rich?"

"Nope."

I gave him a sideways look, and he could see that I didn't believe him.

"Now don't get me wrong," he said, backtracking a little, "I want to find treasure and get rich as much as the next person, but my *primary objective* is not so much about the *getting* – getting the treasure, getting rich. It's about the *finding*. Finding what's been lost. Finding what's been hidden. Finding what doesn't want to be found."

"You must be a very patient and curious person," I concluded.

Chuckling, he replied, "I suppose. Or just a slow learner."

"Can we keep going?"

"Sure."

Chapter 17

For the next few hours, we made our way up and down the beach, me swinging and him scooping. As Emmet had said, people really are pigs, and mostly what we found were pull tabs, pop tops, and wadded up wrappers. Sometimes, though, we'd also find a coin or piece of costume jewelry, which provided us with motivation to keep on swinging.

As the sun began to slide below the horizon, Emmet pointed and said, "Look at that. There's a treasure that you can't put a price on." The sun had turned the sky deep shades of purples, pinks, oranges, and reds and reflected them off of the lake's surface in such a way that we couldn't tell where the sky ended and the lake began. Then as my gaze drifted to the south, I noticed that the sun had turned the rocks and boulders on Goldstone Point to a deep gold, leaving little mystery as to how the point had gotten its name.

The picture painted by that setting sun was so beautiful that I just stood there nearly transfixed, but then a sense of dread suddenly rushed over me. "Uh-oh," I said, "I didn't realize it was getting so late. My folks are going to be really worried about me. It was great to meet you, and thanks for teaching me to metal detect, but I've got to go."

"It was great to meet you, too. Here's your share of the loot," he said, as he held out a few coins.

They had little monetary value, but they represented hours of work as well as a newfound friendship, so I took them with a heartfelt, "Thank you!"

I looked at my phone. I'd put it on silent to better hear the beeps of the metal detector, so I hadn't noticed all of the texts and calls from my parents. "Oh, no... Yep. I'm in trouble." Or, considering what had happened in school that day, "double trouble". Of course, on the other hand, as I had said to myself more than once that day, what did I really have to lose?

Unfortunately, I was about to find out.

Chapter 18

A black sedan pulled into a parking space not far from where Emmet and I were standing. The door on the passenger's side opened, and I heard my dad's voice say, "Get in!"

I looked at Emmet, gave a little shrug, trudged to the car, and got in. "Hey, Dad."

"We texted. We called. Why do we pay for you to have a phone if you won't use it to let us know you're okay?"

"I don't know."

"You. Don't. Know." He looked hard at me. "Well, then I guess that settles it."

"Settles what?"

"You'll find out – when we get home."

Chapter 19

My older sister, Molly, who I affectionately called *The Troll,* had crawled out from beneath her bridge to join us for dinner and was smiling smugly as she silently sat across the table from me. Our parents had been lecturing me for nearly twenty minutes, and my dad finally seemed to be running out of steam. With a sigh, he said, "Okay. Let's recap. Over the course of the past twelve hours, you have made two trips to the principal's office, received a summons from the police, and blatantly defied your parents. As a result, to avoid further consequences, you will adhere to the following terms:

1. You will not leave the house without permission.

2. You will allow a tracker app to be placed on your phone in order for us to know your whereabouts at all times.
3. You will have your phone with you at all times and will answer all of our texts and calls.
4. You will contact the courthouse in order to set up a meeting with the judge.
5. You, and you alone, will be responsible for any and all penalties imposed by the court.
6. You will begin searching for gainful employment.
7. If you do not find gainful employment in what your parents deem is a reasonable amount of time, they will find employment for you.
8. If you fail to abide by these conditions, further consequences will be forthcoming.

Do you understand these terms as I have read them to you?"

"Yes," I answered weakly.

"Then I will make a hard copy of them and

post them on the refrigerator," added my mom. My parents were of the opinion that if something was important, there needed to be a hard copy of it as well as a digital copy. And if it could go on the refrigerator door, so much the better.

My dad looked at me intently. "Is there something that you would like to say to us?"

In hindsight, I probably could have said I was sorry. But I wasn't. So I didn't. Instead, I just sat there trying to think of something that my parents might want to hear. But I couldn't think of anything. So I just sat. Finally, when I could tell that my parents were beginning to lose their patience, I murmured the only thing I could think of: "I don't know."

"Okay. That's what I thought," my dad huffed. "If you think of anything else, let us know. In the meantime, you may go to your room."

I went.

Chapter 20

I had barely gotten into my room when I heard a familiar knock. In answer, I replied with a Dante quote that I thought seemed especially appropriate considering the circumstances: "Abandon all hope, ye who enter here!"

"I fear not, for your mighty sister am I!"

"Then enter at your own risk, Troll, if you must, but you have been warned."

The door opened and in strolled The Troll. Two years older and infinitely wiser, she generally gave pretty good advice when she wasn't being insufferable.

In her best imitation of a toddler's voice she chanted, "Kyle got in trouble, Kyle got — Ouch!"

My baseball glove had mysteriously flown across

the room and hit her squarely in the snout, which soon caused a sneezing fit. "Ah-choo! Ah-choo! Ah-choo!"

"Tell me about it," I lamented.

"Ah-choo!"

"You done?"

"Ah-choo!"

"Guess not."

"Ah-choo! There. I think that's it. Pretty nice toss for someone who didn't make the team."

"Thanks for rubbing it in."

"No problem. That's what I'm here for."

After a pause, she said, "You really should be playing baseball this summer."

"Not my choice. I didn't make the team."

"Actually, it was your choice. How much did you practice? How hard did you try? How bad did you really want to play?"

"I could ask you the same thing. You don't play softball anymore."

"That's different, and you know it. I'm not any good, and you are – or at least you could be. And I've got a summer job. Several, in fact – and you should, too."

Chapter 21

As usual, The Troll was right. She wasn't any good at softball, I could probably be good at baseball, and her services were in high demand during the summer. She taught swim lessons, piano lessons, and flute lessons; she was a music instructor for the summer program at our town's center for fine arts; and when she wasn't working, she played flute and piccolo in the community band and piano for a jazz combo. Even though she was a troll, she was my troll, and I was secretly pretty proud of her.

"Okay, Miss Know-It-All, how do I get out of this mess? I can't stay cooped up in this house all summer."

"And Mom and Dad don't want you to be. Don't you see that they gave you a 'get out of jail free' card?"

I was confused. "What are you talking about?"

"Your ticket out of here is for you to get a summer job, lunkhead!" As she said *lunkhead,* she chucked my baseball glove at me, but as we have already established, my sister's throwing skills were subpar; subsequently, the glove missed me and slammed into the lamp that had previously been resting on my desk. At the sound of the crash, my mother yelled the mantra that had become so familiar in our house over the years: "Kyle! Molly! Get away from each other!"

As she left my room, The Troll whispered, "Remember what I said. Get a job! ANY job!"

Chapter 22

When I woke up the next morning, as usual, the first thing I did was check my phone. As I had feared, there were no messages from my friends. For them, yesterday's last-day-of-school excitement was already a distant memory, and it was on to the next thing: summer vacation – and baseball. As for me, for the first time in memory, it looked like I would be doing summer completely on my own.

I got cleaned up and went downstairs for breakfast. Everyone else in my family had already eaten and left the house, so the kitchen was all mine. Though I was still feeling a little sorry for myself, the prospect of having a ginormous omelet was beginning to brighten my mood. However, when I went to get some eggs, I noticed the result of last night's conversation prominently displayed on our refrigerator door with a baseball shaped magnet. Nice.

As if I needed further reminding, at the top of the page, in big black letters, was typed the following: TERMS OF AGREEMENT. Then, below in smaller letters, it read: BETWEEN KYLE KENNEDY AND HIS PARENTS. As I looked at each term, I began to mentally check them off: Not leaving the house... got it; Tracker on phone... yep, there it is. Yuck! I've got my phone... Hmm... Call the courthouse... Seeing that revved up the butterflies in my stomach. What kind of parent made their kid call the courthouse on their own? Then again, what kind of kid gets into enough trouble to have to call the courthouse in the first place? I was feeling pretty rotten as I punched in the number provided on the summons. Soon, I heard a kind voice that said, "County Clerk of Court, may I help you?"

Chapter 23

"This is Kyle Kennedy, and I've been given a summons?" I managed to blurt out. "I'm supposed to call this number to set up a time to meet with the judge?"

"Yes. I can help you with that. The case number is written at the top of your summons. Can you read it to me, please?"

"9221967."

"Thank you."

After a pause, the lady with the kind voice said, "There's been a cancellation, so you could meet with the judge at ten o'clock this Friday if it works for you."

Friday was just a day away. *Tomorrow.* I contemplated my options. Sometimes it was good to put off the inevitable, and sometimes it was better to just bite the bullet and get it over with. This was one of those times. "That will be fine. Thank you."

"Have you been to the courthouse before?"

"No." Did she think I was a repeat offender or something? But then I remembered that people go to the courthouse for reasons other than meeting with the judge. In fact, I'd be going there myself before too long to get my driver's permit – if my parents would even let me get one after all of this.

"When you come in the front doors, take a left. The judge's chamber is all the way at the end of the hall. If you can't find it, just ask someone. They'll help you."

"Thanks," I said.

"And be sure to show up at your appointed time, because if you don't, there will be a warrant issued for your arrest. You don't want that."

"No. I mean *yes*. Yes, I will come on time," I fumbled. "Thanks."

"Thank you. And have a nice day."

"You, too," I replied, though not nearly as optimistically as the lady with the kind voice.

Chapter 24

With my stomach still full of butterflies, I no longer felt like eating breakfast, so I wandered back to my room to see if there was something there to spark my interest. I was less than an hour into summer vacation, and I was already getting bored, but not bored enough to start considering looking for a *job*.

Since I was supposed to stay at home, the prospects for entertaining myself were somewhat limited: TV? Computer games? Social media? Then my eyes fell on my baseball glove. I guess it wouldn't hurt to throw a few, I thought. Now that I didn't have to worry about getting better or making the team, it seemed like it might be kind of fun.

I grabbed my glove, found the five-gallon

bucket of balls that had been left in the garage untouched since last summer, and went into the backyard. Years earlier, my dad had helped me to set up an old tire in front of a backstop reinforced with a couple layers of old three-quarters inch plywood. I wondered if Dad would tell me to take it down now that I was no longer on the team.

Rectangles of discolored grass extending out from home plate marked the locations where my pitching rubber had been placed over the years. Lined up like shadows of time on the well-manicured lawn, the distance to each rectangle from home plate represented a stage of my pitching career: Thirty-eight feet... Forty-six feet... Fifty-four feet... And finally, in its final resting place, sat my pitching rubber at the high school distance – a whopping sixty feet six inches from home plate.

The discolored rectangles weren't the only visible evidence of my pitching career. A stride's length in front of each rectangle was a slight depression marking where my left foot had landed time after time, pitch after pitch. As the distance between home plate and the rubber increased, so did the distance between the rubber and the depression. As I had grown, so had my stride.

Taking the makeshift mound, I wondered how my stride now would compare to past years' strides. My recent lack of dedication meant that there was no depression at the high school distance to compare it to – though that would soon change.

Chapter 25

From the force of habit, I began going through my pre-throwing stretching regimen. I had always disdained stretching, but it had been a requirement – first of my dad, then of my coaches. Now that it didn't matter to anyone if I stretched or not, I found myself doing it anyway – and it felt kind of good.

When I felt ready, I picked up a severely beaten ball. Years of being chucked into three-quarter inch plywood will do that. I tossed it in the air and caught it. I did it again. And again. The feel of the ball was familiar, yet strange. Never could I remember holding a baseball when there was no pressure, no expectations.

I made an effortless, looping throw. The ball

easily went through the center of the tire and punched the plywood with a satisfying thud. I threw again. *Thud*. And again. *Thud*. Gradually, I began increasing speed. Eventually, the satisfying thuds transformed into resounding *whacks*. I felt good and was actually starting to enjoy myself when I heard I had a text.

I was going to ignore it until I was done, but then I remembered item number three of our agreement: *You will have your phone with you at all times and will answer all of our texts and calls.* I didn't want to violate the agreement on my first day of in-home confinement, so I read the text. It was from my mom: Did you call the courthouse? Did you get a job?

I replied: Yes. No.

I picked up the balls. How did she think I was going to find a job just sitting around the house? As I put the bucket back in the garage, I noticed my fishing rod leaning in the corner where I had left it. I thought to myself, "When in doubt, might as well fish."

I stashed my phone with its newly installed tracker in my bedroom. The butterflies were now long gone, so I made a peanut butter and jelly sandwich and a roast beef and cheese sandwich and threw them in my backpack. There were some chocolate chip cookies on the counter, so I also tossed a pile of them in for good measure. Now that I was well fortified, I hopped on my bike and headed towards the lake.

Chapter 26

When I got to the lake, I was both happy and surprised to see Emmet. He was a couple of hundred yards down the beach but heading my way. Since it would be a bit before he reached me, I decided to make a few casts.

I still had the spinner on from the day before, and it proved to be a good choice. On my second cast, I felt the unmistakable thump of a large fish. I set the hook, my rod doubled over, and my drag sang.

The fish continued to take line for what seemed like an eternity. There wasn't anything I could do but to hold on. Suddenly, it turned and charged back towards me. I cranked on my reel as fast as I could, trying to keep the slack out of my line. And then he jumped. In a blinding spectacle of light and water, I could see my lure fly one way and a monster musky the other.

Line limp, heart pounding, adrenaline pumping, I stood like a statue, gazing with unbelieving eyes into the depths of the now silent still water where my fish was undoubtedly enjoying his newfound freedom. It may have just been my imagination, but I could have sworn that I could hear him laughing at me.

Chapter 27

"Tough break. That fish is the king of the lake."

The sound of Emmet's voice brought me back to reality. "Yeah, but at least I got to see him."

"There is that," he acknowledged.

"Doing any good?" I asked, looking at the detector by his side.

"Just modern coins and one silver ring – and pull tabs!" he laughed.

"No gold?"

"Nope, the beach has been hit pretty hard by other detectorists, but in another week or so the water will be warm enough for me to start water detecting, and then I should start finding some of the yellow stuff."

"Why's that?" I asked, my curiosity piqued.

"There's no mystery to it, really. People come to the beach on a hot sunny day, slather themselves in suntan lotion, go for a swim, and that's the last they see of their rings. Suntan lotion and pruny swim fingers are a deadly combination for rings."

"So you're saying that if I'm ever wearing a big gold ring, unless you're around to help me find it, I should take it off before going for a swim," I said jokingly.

"Actually, if you ever have a big gold ring, it would probably be better if you'd just leave it at home. I have a feeling that a lot of the rings lost on the beach are from folks putting them on their towels for safekeeping, forgetting about them, and then when they shake out their towels when they get ready to leave, they send them flying.

Chapter 28

I looked wistfully at Emmet's metal detector. "I wish I had one of those. Then I wouldn't need to find a summer job. I could just scoop up piles of money and jewelry from the sand."

Emmet went into one of his roaring fits of laughter. I didn't know what was so funny, but as before, his laughter was so contagious that I couldn't help joining in. After he was done and had about caught his breath, he said, "Very few people can make a job out of metal detecting. It's a great hobby, but I've been doing this for years, and I have yet to meet anyone who could consistently find enough to pay for their machines and batteries – let alone their time. I've read about a few folks who have hit it big, found a buried treasure or something, and maybe you've read about them, too;

but even then, finding and keeping are two different things."

Emmet must have been able to see my disappointment because he quickly said, "I'll tell you what. If you've got a few minutes, I'll let you in on a secret for how you can find a little sumthin-sumthin on your own – without a metal detector."

Chapter 29

I was incredulous. How could a person find anything without a metal detector? Even I knew that I needed a metal detector in order to find metal – or at least I thought I did. But what if I didn't? "Okay, how can I find 'a little sumthin-sumthin' without a metal detector?"

"Have you ever panned for gold?"

"No."

"Have you ever watched someone pan for gold, on TV or something?"

"I guess. Maybe. I don't know. I really can't remember." His line of questioning was starting to get old, and it was becoming apparent that I might have to wallow through a bunch of boring in order to find the "little sumthin-sumthin" he'd been talking about.

"So I'm guessing that you have no idea how panning for gold works?"

"Emmet Arnold, you are correct. Ladies and gentlemen, we have a winner! Tell us, Chuck, what do we have for Emmet? Emmet has just won... A NEW CAR!" It was now my turn to go into fits of laughter.

Emmet looked at me like I was from another planet. Apparently, he wasn't used to hanging out with fourteen-year-olds.

"Are you done?"

"Yes," I said, trying to get my breath.

"Good. Now, listen carefully. I'm going to teach you about gold panning."

"There's no gold to pan here," I said obstinately. "Why do I need to know about gold panning?"

"Because that is how you're going to find 'a little sumthin-sumthin.' If you know a better way, have at it. You don't need me."

I feared that I had hurt Emmet's feelings. "Sorry. I'm just confused, but if you think it will help, then tell me how to pan for gold."

Chapter 30

Regaining some of his enthusiasm, Emmet began, "When you pan for gold, you find a place where gold can be found, scoop up a heaping pile of sand and gravel, and swish it around in your pan along with some water; as you swish the conglomeration around in your pan, the lighter materials will gradually rise to the top, and the heavier materials (like gold) will eventually sink to the bottom. To get to the gold, you just gradually let the lighter materials slip out of your pan until all that you have left is the gold."

He could see that I still wasn't convinced that knowing how to pan for gold was going to help me find any gold in our lake, so he tossed a fist-sized rock onto the beach where the water met the sand

and asked, "What do you see?"

"A rock."

"What else?

"Sand."

"What else?"

"Waves."

"What are they doing?"

"I don't know."

"Wrong answer. Keep looking."

I kept looking at the waves. They were lapping at the shore, gently rocking the sand and gravel back and forth. Then I saw something remarkable. The fist-sized rock was slowly being engulfed, disappearing as though it were sinking in quicksand.

A light came on in my head, and I shouted, "The lake is like a giant gold pan!"

"Ladies and gentlemen, we have a winner! Just like in a gold pan, the wave action in the lake causes the light materials to rise and the heavy materials to sink."

"But Emmet," I asked, "how do you get rid of the sand and gravel from the lake? You can't just dump it out like you do with a pan."

"No, you can't, and in some lakes that's a bigger problem than in others. You see, some lakes just have sand or mud bottoms, and in those lakes, the gold just keeps sinking until it's out of reach – for me, at least. In other lakes, like this one, there's something called hardpan. It's a dense mixture of blue clay and hard packed gravel that prevents gold from sinking further. If you can reach hardpan, you can reach gold – and silver, and anything else that people have lost or thrown away over the years, some valuable, some not so much."

"So how do I get to all of that good stuff you're talking about?"

"To find the good stuff, you gotta dig deep – sometimes really deep." He looked around and motioned for me to come closer. I did. With a voice just above a whisper, he said, "And to do that, you'll need a treasure sifter."

Chapter 31

As it turned out, the contraption that Emmet called a treasure sifter was nothing more than a two foot by three-foot rectangle of five-eighths inch wire mesh that had been fastened to a two-by-four frame. Emmet brought one from his van along with a shovel and showed me how to use it. First, he positioned it so about a third of it was on the beach and two-thirds of it was in the water. Next, he shoveled a few scoops of sand from the water's edge onto the wire. Then he vigorously sloshed the sifter up and down and side to side, letting all the sand and small rocks filter through. Finally, he used one hand to sort through what was left on the screen to see if he'd found anything good. Deceptively simple. Incredibly effective.

"Can I try?" I asked.

"Sure. In fact, if you like it, you're welcome to use it and that old shovel as much as you like. Just one thing, though, you have to make sure to fill in all of your holes. When you're done, I don't want to see any sign that you've been here."

I nodded.

"And another thing, starting with this weekend, things are going to get busy around here. Only sift in the mornings and stop at 8:00 AM."

"Okay. But why can't I do it when people are around? Sifting isn't illegal, is it?"

"No. It's not illegal, and we want to keep it that way. If you leave big old holes around and make a mess of things, people aren't going to like it. Then it might become illegal."

"Okay. I see what you mean about the holes, but that doesn't explain why I can't sift when people are around…"

"Lots of reasons," he said gruffly. "First, people are nosy. Do you want a bunch of people snooping into your business? Asking all sorts of questions? Bothering you when you're trying to work? Second, people are crooked." He saw the surprised look on my face. "Yes, crooked. For instance, what do you think they're going to say when they see that gold ring seem to magically appear on your sifter screen? 'Oh, that's so nice for you?' Nope. They're going to say 'Hey! That's the ring I lost last summer! Give it here!' Finally, who needs more competition? It's not like this isn't something that everyone can do. Who needs other folks finding our stuff? And who needs other folks making a mess of the beach and making things a mess for us? Nope. Better off just flying under the radar. Be inconspicuous. Now give it a try. I want to see how you do."

Chapter 32

Shovel some sand, dump it into the sifter. Shovel some sand, dump it into the sifter. Shake-shake-slosh… Shake-shake-slosh… Scan the sifter screen to see if there is anything good. Dump the contents of the sifter that can't fit through the screen. Repeat.

As it turned out, sifting was both easier and harder than it looked. The process itself was simple, efficient, and almost elegant; but the shoveling, dumping, shaking, and sloshing was dirty, wet, grueling work. I thought I was in good physical shape, but it wasn't long before I was beginning to feel some soreness in my arms, legs, and back. I'd broken a pretty good sweat and was getting more than a little winded when I decided to take a break.

Leaning on the shovel I questioned Emmet, "Are you sure this works? I haven't found anything yet but rocks and broken glass."

"Be patient."

"I know, 'You gotta dig deep to get to the good stuff.'"

"That's right. You'll start finding iron and maybe some coins as you get closer to the hardpan. After you hit hardpan – who knows?"

I went back to work, and as usual, Emmet was right. Nails, bolts, and unidentifiable chunks of rust-encrusted iron started showing up. Then, as I pawed through the rocks too big to fit through the screen, I saw a dark gray disc. Thrilled with the prospect of having finally found something worthwhile, I reached for it and shouted triumphantly, "Hey! I think I found something good!"

Almost instantly, I found myself with one of Emmet's giant paws firmly clamped over my mouth and the other across the back of my head. He twisted my head so I could look him in the eyes. His voice was cold and measured. "Don't you ever do that again. If you find something, good. Put it away and keep doing what you're doing like nothing happened. You don't know who's watching. You don't know who's listening. Understand?"

I nodded my head.

"Good."

Chapter 33

The gray disc turned out to be a 1942 Washington quarter, and according to Emmet, it was worth around four or five dollars depending on the current price of silver.

Though slightly shaken by Emmet's stern warning, I was not to be deterred. With newfound enthusiasm, I redoubled my efforts; and as Emmet had predicted, when I reached hardpan, the finds really started piling up. Patiently, he provided me with the name of each coin as I plucked it from the screen: Mercury dime... buffalo nickel... wheat penny... Barber quarter... Roosevelt dime... another Mercury dime... another buffalo nickel...

Much too quickly, the finds started dwindling, and Emmet finally said, "I think this hole is all played out."

"Now what?" I asked.

"You dig another hole right next to it. Put the sifter over the top of the old one so you can fill it up as you go."

And that is how it went: Me sifting and Emmet supervising. It was hard work, but it was also addicting. With each scoopful, we never knew what the sifting sand would reveal. It might be junk, it might be a silver coin, and it might be... gold.

Chapter 34

Eventually, as the morning wore on, my growling stomach began to get in the way of my enthusiasm, so I said to Emmet, "I brought a couple of sandwiches. Do you want one?"

"What kind?"

"Peanut butter and jelly or roast beef."

"Are they cut in half?"

"Actually, they are."

"In that case, how about we each take half of each."

I headed back up the beach to where I'd left my rod and backpack, and when I returned, I saw that Emmet had set up a couple of camping chairs with a water bottle stuffed in each chair's beverage holder.

"Might as well be comfortable," he said, as he cautiously settled his large frame into one of the chairs. I couldn't help but smile a little. It was painfully obvious that Emmet was all too familiar with collapsing chairs.

Food always tastes better outdoors, especially after a morning of hard work. We had finished both sandwiches and were starting on the cookies when I noticed the bag containing our keepers lying near our feet.

"How much money do you suppose this is worth?" I asked as I reached for the bag and began to open it.

"Wait! Don't examine your finds on the beach. Next thing you know, you'll have lost them again. History is full of treasures that have been lost, found, and lost again. Keep your treasure in the bag until you have a safe place to look it over."

Chapter 35

After the last cookie was gone, Emmet stood, released a giant five-second belch, and announced in a voice brimming with contentment, "That was an excellent lunch. Thank you."

"You're welcome, but it was only sandwiches and cookies."

"Nothing wrong with that. They were the best sandwiches and cookies that I've had in ages. The trouble with your generation is that you take things for granted. You don't appreciate things. Look at you, for instance. I don't know much about you, but I know that you have someone who cares enough about you to provide you with food, clothes, and a roof over your head. In fact, they must think an awful lot of you to take the time to make you some cookies."

I thought Mr. Burns could give long lectures, but I soon found that his were nothing compared to Emmet's.

"Not only that, but you're sitting here with your full belly enjoying a million-dollar view with nothing more to do than dig in the sand the rest of the afternoon if it pleases you, and all you can do is complain that you ONLY had sandwiches and cookies for lunch. You, my friend, are spoiled. Spoiled rotten. You obviously don't have a job or play summer ball or you wouldn't be here. Lazy, unmotivated, and unappreciative. Am I wrong?"

"I dunno."

"Sure you do.

Chapter 36

By the time Emmet was through lecturing and we'd gotten back to sifting, all traces of our earlier activity had been washed away. "Where shall we start?" I asked.

"It probably doesn't matter. Our last hole must have been near where we left the bucket of trash and shovel, so let's just go down a few yards and start there."

I did as I was told. This time, though, when I started digging, Emmet began working the sifter. When I gave him a questioning look, he said with a twinkle in his eye, "It will go faster this way. As slow and lazy as you are, you'll never find any gold at the rate you're going."

For the rest of the afternoon, we traded off

digging and sifting. And of course, Emmet was right, it did go much faster, and we did find a lot of keepers: a large handful of modern coins, a slightly smaller handful of older coins, a silver ring that was missing a stone, a toy sheriff's badge, and some costume jewelry.

It wasn't only metal that we found, though. People lose all sorts of things, and many of those things aren't made of metal. We found marbles of all types and sizes, broken bits of colorful glass worn smooth from the waves and sand, and old plastic toys in various states of deterioration.

But with all the things we were finding, there was still one thing missing.

"Why aren't we finding any gold?" I asked.

"Because we just haven't dug where it's at yet."

"Well, where is it at? You said if we found hardpan, we'd find gold. Where's the gold?"

"Maybe if you would do more looking and less complaining, you'd find some."

My eyes flew to the sifter. There, partially covered in sand, was the unmistakable glow of gold.

Chapter 37

The sight of gold nearly caused me to lose control and let out a huge triumphant shout, but then I remembered how it had felt to have Emmet's hand clamped over my mouth; so instead, fighting back excitement, I just casually used a trembling finger to nudge the object a couple of times. Sand fell away, and gradually the item's identity was revealed: a man's giant gold class ring.

Emmet smiled and said, "Why don't you put that in the bag, and we'll call it a day?"

Remembering the lesson about not attracting attention, I nonchalantly reached down and grabbed the ring just like I was grabbing a beat-up penny or piece of junk. As I lifted it from the screen, I noticed that it was surprisingly heavy for its size, and the smooth, cool metal almost felt alive in my hand.

"You sure I can't just put it in my pocket?" I asked.

"Put it in the bag."

Reluctantly, I did.

"You may not think it is a big deal, but if the wrong people are watching, what then? No, better just to muddle along and make it look like you're not finding much."

"So what do we do now? Where do we put the sifter, shovel, the bag of you-know-what, and the rest of the stuff?"

"How about this. I'm starting to get a little up there in years and could use a partner. I realize you don't know me very well, and I don't know you very well, but if you want, each day when we're done, I can store the equipment, sort the coins and other keepers, and give you market value for them the next day. In cash. How does that sound?"

On one hand, I knew there was a real possibility that I'd never see Emmet or any of the keepers that we'd found again if I let him take them; but on the other hand, even if he looked like he was pushing sixty or so, Emmet was obviously big and strong enough to take the stuff we'd found if he wanted to; but on another hand, I wouldn't have found any of the stuff anyway if it hadn't been for Emmet and his sifter and willingness to teach me; so was any of it even really mine anyway?

"Okay. Sounds good. I have an appointment tomorrow morning, but I should be able to be here sometime after lunch."

"I hope your appointment goes well."

"Me, too."

Chapter 38

When I got home, I was pleased to see that neither of my parents' cars were in the driveway. At least for the time being, it looked like my little ruse of leaving my phone behind in my room may have worked. Feeling pretty smug, I opened the front door, and all my hopeful thoughts went flying out the window.

In the middle of our living room, wearing a malevolent grin, stood The Troll. From the looks of the candy wrappers, crumpled potato chip bag, and empty bowl of ice cream, she obviously had been waiting for me for quite some time – brooding, plotting, planning. Now that her quarry had entered her lair, I knew she would soon unleash the evil she had so carefully crafted.

Slowly, deliberately, she raised her spindly little dinosaur arms with their puny little dinosaur hands. One held my phone, the other THE TERMS OF AGREEMENT. This was bad. Really bad. Still smiling, The Troll cocked her head to one side, and with a sickeningly sweet voice chirped, "Hello, Kyle, did you have a nice day?"

"What do you want?" I replied, cutting to the chase.

She put a hand on my shoulder and chided, "Come, come, Kyle. You sound so suspicious. I only want you to help me help you help yourself. Is that such a bad thing?"

I brushed her hand away. "You only want to help *your*self."

"That's not true," she replied, trying to sound hurt. "I'm your big sister, and I only want to look out for you. Can't you see that I want what's best for you?"

"Then give me my phone and keep quiet about things that aren't your business."

"Business..." she said thoughtfully. "Well, if business is what you want, then maybe we should conduct a little business." She plopped herself down on the sofa and put her feet up. "I'll tell you what I'll do. You do all of my house and yard chores, and I'll protect you by forgetting what I know about where you were (or weren't) today. Deal?"

Even though The Troll's bloodsucking protection racket was only a thinly veiled excuse for blackmail and extortion, in hindsight, I probably got off pretty easy considering the amount of damage she could have done. With my impending court date, I didn't need to take any unnecessary chances.

Chapter 39

When I awoke the next morning, it was hard for me to believe that it was already Friday. The Friday that would decide my fate. *Fateful Friday.* Ugh. Thankfully, my dad agreed to take time off from work to go to the courthouse with me. Calling the clerk was one thing, but actually going to the courthouse and appearing before a judge was a whole new level of scary.

When we got there, he dropped me off out front and said, "You go on in and find out where we need to go. I'll try to find a safe place to park." I gave my dad a worried look, and with a surprising show of compassion, he said, "It'll be alright. As long as you keep moving forward, things have a way of working out." So with more than a little trepidation, I stepped out of the vehicle and zombie-like began trudging to meet my fate.

Our county courthouse was built somewhere in the middle of the nineteenth century. Many people in our town thought it had a stately look to it with its unadorned limestone brickwork and rows upon rows of windows; however, as I hiked the twenty-two steps to its front doors, the only words that I could think of to describe the mammoth, boxlike structure about to swallow me were words like *threatening… ominous…* and *foreboding.*

Inside wasn't much better: musty, gloomy, and smelling like the boys' locker room. It was a busy place, but most of the people seemed cheerless, anxious, and apprehensive. Some sat silently in the few available chairs, others aimlessly leaned against a wall that sometime in the last century had been painted institutional green, but most stood patiently in one of several lines.

I looked around for the clerk's office. I'd taken a virtual tour the night before, so I sort of had an idea of which direction to go. It wasn't long until I saw that one of the long lines led to a lady behind a counter with a sign that said "Clerk of Court" over her head. Bingo.

I joined the line and became one of the cheerless in a long line of cheerlessness. I'd almost reached the lady at the counter when my dad showed up. "Sorry it took so long, but I had to park nearly three blocks away."

"That's okay. You haven't missed anything," I said, and then I realized that for the first time in a long time, it was the truth. He hadn't missed anything. Over the past few years, he'd missed ballgames, track meets, concerts, plays, and musicals; but that day at the courthouse, that day when I knew he was disappointed in me, was embarrassed by me, and wished he could be anywhere else but with me, he was there. He hadn't missed a thing.

Chapter 40

The lady at the clerk's counter was very pleasant and helpful and could well have been the one I had talked to on the phone. Surprisingly, after I told her who I was, she said, "It's your lucky day. The judge has already looked at your case and has asked that you meet with him in his chambers." Pointing over our shoulders, she said, "If you go down the hall right behind you, you'll see a sign that says *Judge Matheson* and a couple of chairs. Have a seat, and someone will be with you shortly."

We thanked her and did as we were told. The door with the judge's name on it wasn't hard to find, and the chairs were vacant. So far, so good.

"What do you think he'll say?" I asked, taking one of the chairs.

My dad, taking the other chair, replied, "I don't know. Just be polite and try telling the truth for a change."

That was good advice, but though being polite had never been a problem for me, telling the truth was. For as long as I could remember, I'd always thought, "Why tell the truth when a lie is so much more interesting?"

The lady at the clerk's counter had been correct. We had only been seated a couple of minutes when the heavy oak door opened and another lady stepped out and said, "The judge will see you now."

Chapter 41

The judge's chambers were not what I expected. No shelves straining from the weight of thick, dusty books, no ancient hardwood floors worn smooth from use, and no dark leather chairs or old oak tables. Instead, everything was bright, light, and airy. In addition, the most prominent feature in the room, the person I assumed was the judge himself, appeared to only be in his thirties or forties, wore a red shirt and black tie rather than a robe, and as he stood in the middle of the room, he appeared to be nearly seven-feet tall.

My astonishment must have been apparent because the man took a couple of steps towards us, shook our hands, and said, "Hello. I'm Judge Matheson. I see from your expression that my chambers aren't exactly as you expected them to be – nor am I."

"No, sir. I mean no, *Your Honor*," I stammered.

"Don't feel bad," he said. "You're not the first to be a bit taken aback. Things aren't always the way we picture them or the way they're portrayed on TV. Have a seat, and let's get started."

He sat behind his desk, which was bare except for a laptop, and we took the two chairs in front of it.

"Kyle," he said, "I've looked over your case, and before I issue a sentence, I have a couple of questions for you."

Uh-oh, I thought. Here it comes…

Chapter 42

Judge Matheson leaned forward in his chair. Even sitting, his height was imposing. Then he began with a serious, rather ominous voice, "First, are you sorry for what you have done?"

"Yes. Very sorry."

"Sorry for what you did? Or sorry that now you must face the consequences for what you did?"

I squirmed in my chair. "I don't know. Both, I guess."

"That's what I thought. Second question, what are your plans for this summer? Are you playing sports? Are you working?"

I got the feeling that things weren't going well for me. I shifted a bit more in my chair, glanced at my dad, and then gave the answer that I thought would benefit me the most and still wasn't too far from the truth: "I'm working."

Surprised, my dad turned towards me and said, "I didn't know you found a job."

"Yeah," I mumbled. "I got one yesterday."

"Good," said Judge Matheson. "Where is your place of employment?"

Before I had time to think, "Arnold's Salvage and Recovery" came out of my mouth.

"Hmmm… I don't believe I've heard of that business," mused the judge.

"It's new," I said weakly. Then I quickly added, "That's why they needed help."

"Well that worked out well for you then because now you have a means for paying back your debt to society."

"Debt to society?"

"Yes, debt to society. Kyle, in light of your blatant disrespect for authority and disregard for the well-being of your fellow human beings, I have sentenced you to pay a fine of $1500."

Chapter 43

After the court appointment, it was a quiet car ride back to my house. All my dad said when he dropped me off was, "I hope your job pays well."

"Me, too," I said under my breath. Then I added, "Dad? Thanks." I think I caught him off guard because he didn't seem to know what to say. He just got out of the car, walked around to my side, and gave me a hug. A hug. Right in the middle of the street. It was kind of weird, since I couldn't remember the last time that I'd gotten a hug from either of my parents; but in spite of that, I have to confess that it was kind of cool, too.

Without either of us saying a word, he got back in the car and left for work, and I decided that I'd better pack some lunch and get to my "job", too.

Chapter 44

"Fifteen hundred dollars? That's a lot of money for a person your age," said Emmet as he scooped up a quarter that his metal detector had located. "Are you going to pay it yourself, or are your parents going to bail you out?"

"I'm going to try to pay it."

"Do you have that kind of money?"

"No."

"How long do you have to come up with it?"

"It's due July 1, so I guess about four weeks."

Emmet's forehead furrowed. "Then by my rough math, you're either going to have to get a real job, or you're going to need to find around fifty dollars' worth of 'treasure' every day for a month in order to pay it off. Here." He handed me the quarter that he'd just found. "You can start with this."

"Thanks a lot. That's a real big help," I said sarcastically. "Got a few thousand more where that came from?"

Emmet smiled. "No, but I do have this." He handed me an envelope. "There's twenty-seven dollars in there. Your share of yesterday's take. It's not a lot, but it's a start. And since it was your first gold find, you can also have this." He gave me the class ring. "You can keep it, pawn it, or sell it – or I can give you $200 for it."

Needless to say, I was surprised on several counts. "Thanks!" I said, taking the ring. Now it was my turn to do some quick math. If I could average $230 per day, I could have my fine paid off in a week! But what were the chances of finding a large gold ring every day? And even if I did, I'd have to share half with Emmet since we were partners. I almost said that I'd take the cash, but then I took a closer look at the ring and noticed "Elvin H.S." printed on the side and became curious. Where was Elvin? Who was the student that went there? When and how did he lose his ring?

I needed the money, but I wasn't ready to part

with the ring just yet. "Emmet, I think I'll just hang on to the ring for a while until I decide what to do with it."

"Suit yourself, but you better get to work. After today, you can only sift early mornings. Remember?"

To tell the truth, I'd forgotten, but I didn't need Emmet to know how irresponsible I was. "Yeah. I remember. Only until 8:00 starting tomorrow, right?"

"Right. So get here as early as you can." He pointed to where the sifter and shovel were resting several yards down the beach. "I'll leave those where you can find them like I did today. If I don't happen to be around when you start, don't worry. I'll be back before you're done so we can settle up. Any questions?"

"No. I don't think so."

"Okay, then. Good luck."

I wandered down the beach. As I approached the sifter and shovel, I noticed that in the sand next to them were a few crudely scrawled words – the same words that I would come to find scrawled next to them every morning: DIG DEEP.

Chapter 45

For the next couple of weeks, my days followed a rather predictable schedule: Wake up at 4:30. Walk to the beach. Sift until 8:00. Walk home. Eat breakfast. Nap until noon. Eat lunch. Do any chores that my parents left sticky-noted to the fridge door. Throw for an hour or so. Run a few miles. Swim to cool off. Walk home. Shower. Eat supper. Fish until dark. Go home. Sleep. Repeat.

Our treasure finds had been consistent if not spectacular. Each day, we usually found three or four heaping handfuls of modern coins, a small handful of old coins, a piece or two of silver jewelry, and occasionally a piece of small gold jewelry. All in all, minus the class ring, my share of the profits was only averaging about $35 per day, which was concerning since that would place me well short of what I needed to reach my goal.

Though no other class rings had turned up, it didn't take much detective work on my part to identify the owner of the ring that we did find. Upon further inspection, the initials W.D. and 1957 were stamped on it along with Elvin H.S. A quick internet search provided me with a list of names from Elvin High School's graduating class of 1957, and only one name had the initials W.D. – Wayne Dunbar.

From what I could find online, it seems that in high school Wayne was involved in baseball, football, basketball, track, band, and the glee club. He was also the lead in at least one musical. Two years after graduating, he left for Europe and started businesses in Germany, France, and England. He retired in 2001 with an estimated net worth of over four million dollars. After retiring, he returned to the United States and now apparently resides happily in California. He has four children, twelve grandchildren, and six great-grandchildren.

The money that I could have gotten from selling the ring would have been nice, but now that I knew who the owner was, selling it just didn't seem right.

I had never been one to listen too closely to my conscience, but for some reason, with the finding of that ring, I began to feel differently about things. Maybe it was all of the time I was spending alone without my friends as an audience, maybe it was all of the exercise, maybe I was just finally growing up. I don't know, but I do know that eventually I couldn't even bring myself to look at that ring without feeling guilty. I knew I had something that didn't belong to me, and I knew I wouldn't feel good about myself until I got it back to its owner. So I boxed it up with a note explaining how I'd found it and sent it to Wayne Dunbar in California.

Chapter 46

Usually, Emmet and I pretty much had the beach to ourselves. Occasionally there might be an early morning jogger or fisherman, but for the most part, we were left to do our plundering in peace: Emmet swinging his metal detector, and me at the sifter. Then one morning as I was kneeling at my work, a shadow fell across the sifter. When I looked up to see what was blocking my light, a boy about my age was standing above me wearing one of the biggest smiles I'd ever seen. "Hi," he said, still grinning. "Whatcha doin'?"

I gave him the standard line that I gave most people who interrupted my work, "Just messing around in the sand."

"Why?"

"Sometimes I find things like pop tops, pull tabs, nails, broken glass – stuff that people have lost or thrown away. I like to keep the beach clean."

He wasn't buying it. "Maybe you're also trying to find some old coins, rings, and jewelry, too, huh?"

"Maybe," I said vaguely, not wanting to lie, but not wanting to give away that that was *exactly* what I was trying to find.

"Can I help? You can keep everything. I just want to try it. It looks like fun."

His friendliness seemed genuine, and his enthusiasm was infectious. Besides, I had hardly talked to anyone my age all summer and was feeling a bit lonely, so a little companionship along with some free labor sounded pretty good. "Sure. There isn't much to it. Just shovel, sift, look to see what you've found, and do it again."

"Great! I've got this!" he said, reaching for the shovel.

And he did. Until the eight o'clock stop time, he dug hole after hole while I identified each of his finds – much like Emmet had done for me on my first day. When Emmet showed up, I was a little surprised that he didn't grumble about me letting someone in on our treasure hunting secrets. Instead, he just gave my new friend a long look and said, "You're Margorie's grandson, aren't you?"

"Yes, sir. I'm staying with her for the summer."

Emmet gave a little smile. "Thought so. This place is just full of coincidences," he mused. "Now help me put this stuff away, and we'll call it a day."

We packed the van and gave Emmet our finds. "See you tomorrow," said Emmet.

As we watched him drive away, I said, "You want some breakfast? My house is only a couple of blocks from here."

"You bet! I'm starved!"

"Did you walk or ride a bike here?"

"Actually, I drove," he said, and pointed to a sleek blue and white ski boat tied to a dock maybe sixty yards or so down the beach. "We can take a ride in it after breakfast if you want. It belongs to my grandma, but she lets me use it whenever I want."

"Nice! Say, what's your name, anyway? Mine's Kyle Kennedy."

"Mine's Joey Jefferson."

Chapter 47

Joey Jefferson… As we walked to my house, I kept wondering where I'd seen that name before. It seemed familiar, but I couldn't quite place it. Then Joey said, "You play baseball?"

Of course! That was it. His was the unfamiliar name on the baseball roster. I suppose I had good reason to be a bit jealous of him: getting to stay at a house on the lake all summer, having a great boat to use whenever he wanted, and to top it all off, taking my place on *my* school's baseball team – but I wasn't. If he took my spot on the team, he probably deserved it, and it wasn't his fault that his grandma was nice and let him stay with her and use her boat. So in answer to his question, I just said, "I dunno."

"What do you mean you don't know?"

I shrugged. "Like I said. I don't know."

He let it drop and looking at his dirty clothes said, "I'm kind of a mess. You sure your mom wants me in your house?"

"She'd be okay with it since you're a guest, but maybe you should go around to the backyard to be on the safe side. You'll find some lawn chairs there. I'll be out in a minute."

Chapter 48

When I stepped out the backdoor with some ham, egg, and cheese biscuits that I'd heated up from the freezer, Joey was standing by my pitching tire.

"Looks like this thing has gotten a lot of use," he said.

"Some." I handed him his sandwich. "What would you like to drink? Water, milk, or orange juice?"

"Orange juice sounds good. Mind if I try out your bullpen?"

"Sure. There's a bucket of balls in the garage, and you'll find a couple of gloves there, too. One should fit."

Before the second glass was full, I heard "Whump! Whump! Whump!" It wasn't the loud

"Thwack!" that I'd gotten used to hearing when I threw, but I could tell by the sound that he still had plenty of speed. If he also had control, he was probably pretty good.

It was at that moment that I came to a realization: *I* was pretty good, too – really good, in fact. My workouts had improved my speed, control, and stamina. With a twinge of regret, I knew that I was throwing the best that I ever had. It didn't really matter, though, since I didn't make the team and would have been kicked off it even if I had. Actions have consequences. No one would ever know or care that over the course of the past few weeks my fastball had already punched two holes in the side of our garage, and even though shiny new plywood now covered the old, I knew it wouldn't last long.

Chapter 49

I brought the glasses of orange juice out, and we relaxed in the chairs while we ate.

"These breakfast biscuits are really good," said Joey. "Be sure to thank your mom for me."

I smiled, "Actually, you can thank me."

"*You* made them?"

"Sure. I've become a pretty good cook this summer if I do say so myself. So you're a pitcher?"

"Yeah. Pitcher and shortstop." Then he looked at me incredulously, "You obviously have practiced more than you're letting on. If you don't mind me asking, what's the deal? Why aren't you playing?"

"The long story is too long, but the short story is that I just wasn't good enough at tryouts. Speaking of tryouts, I didn't see you there."

"I wasn't. I feel kind of bad about that. I wasn't done with school when tryouts took place, so I couldn't make it."

"Then how'd you make the team?" I could tell the direction of the conversation was making him kind of uncomfortable. I didn't want to make him feel bad, so I hurriedly said, "You don't have to tell me if you don't want to. It's really none of my business."

"No. It's alright." He took a deep breath and let it out. Then he said, "Okay, so here's the deal. Coach saw me playing some travel ball last fall and told me if I was ever in the area, I should let him know. So when I learned that I'd be here this summer, I did."

"And now you're playing baseball for my school – even though you don't go there."

"Right."

I leaned back in my chair, put my hands behind my head, and in my best detective voice said, "Well, that is *interesting*."

"I know. It sounded like a good idea at the time, but now I'm not so sure."

Chapter 50

I'd heard of coaches bringing in ringers, but I never thought it'd happen at our school. But then I thought to myself that maybe we didn't know the whole story, that maybe everything really was on the up and up – and even if it wasn't, what could be done about it now?

Joey, who had been so upbeat all morning, was now looking about as sad as a daisy in an April snowstorm. I didn't know what to say to the kid who had done something about as dumb as I had. Finally, after several awkward moments of silence, I just said, "Don't worry about it. Things will work out."

"Maybe."

I gave him a conciliatory smile and said, "So

other than being a big-time ringer with a guilty conscience, how is baseball going?"

"Alright, I guess. We've won about half of our varsity games so far, and the JV is undefeated."

"Have you been bumped up to varsity much?" I asked. In our school, younger players often played both JV and varsity in order to gain as much experience as possible, and I just assumed that Joey was doing the same. Occasionally an incoming ninth grader was so talented that they would only suit varsity, but not very often. So you can imagine my surprise when Joey's face got red and he mumbled, "Yeah, I've been playing some varsity."

"Get out of here!" I exclaimed. "You're ONLY playing varsity, aren't you! And from the look on your face, I bet you've been playing a lot! You must be really good. I guess I should have known that since Coach recruited you."

Trying to change the subject, Joey asked, "Do you want to play a little catch?"

"You bet I do. I need to see what you've got that has Coach so excited."

Chapter 51

We spent the rest of the morning playing catch, hanging out, and pretty much just goofing off the way only teenagers can. It was the first day all summer that I'd hung out with someone other than Emmet, and even though sitting with him was fun, it wasn't the same as doing things with someone my own age.

It didn't take long to find out that Joey was a good pitcher. Really good, in fact. I could see why Coach had him on varsity. As I suspected, his fastball wasn't super fast, but he had a curveball that was nobody's business. I pretended to bat a bit as he tossed to the tire, and each time he threw his curve, I found myself bailing out of the batter's box, only to have the ball arc right back into the center of the strike zone.

"With a curve like that, I can see why you're on varsity," I observed.

"Thanks. My dad taught me. He used to play in the pros."

My jaw dropped. "You've. Got. To. Be. Kidding." I said in disbelief. This was almost too much. Not only did this kid have a boat, lake house, and my spot on the team, he also had a dad that was a former professional baseball player. "Your dad pitched in the pros?"

"No. He was a catcher."

"Wow. Just... Wow."

Suddenly, Joey looked at his phone and exclaimed, "I've got to go! I told my grandma that I'd be home for lunch, and if I don't leave now, I'm going to be late. Sorry. Maybe we can take the boat out another time?"

"Sure. What about this afternoon? It'll be warmer then, anyway."

"Uh..." he said sheepishly.

"Let me guess. You've got a game?"

"Yeah."

"No worries. Some other time," I said, trying to sound upbeat.

"For sure! Thanks again! This was great! See you tomorrow!" And he was gone.

Did I hear him right? Did he say that he'd see me tomorrow?

Chapter 52

I had heard him right. When I got to the lake the next morning, he was already at work, shoveling, sifting, and separating the good from the garbage. "I hope you don't mind me starting without you," he said. "I woke up early and couldn't get back to sleep, so I just got up and came on over. Emmet was already here and set me up."

"I don't mind at all! Found anything yet?"

"Not much. Just a few modern coins and junk, but this is addictive! You never know what's going to be in the next scoop!"

I understood what he was talking about. I'd said the same thing. It *was* addictive. Even after a couple of weeks of waking up at o'dark hundred, I still felt a rush of adrenaline with each scoop of the shovel

– and not just because I needed the money. It really was a lot of fun.

Eventually, Emmet made his way over to check on us. "Gentlemen, I think it's time we take a break."

"What? Why?" we said simultaneously.

"Because I think it's time that we have a little talk."

Joey and I looked at each other. What could Emmet want to talk to us about? He had set up three lawn chairs for us, and after we were seated, he cleared his throat. "Let me begin by saying that sometimes people will do things when they're young, scared, and stupid that they'd never do under other circumstances, and I'm sorry for any pain that I may have caused you or your families." I was about to ask a question, but Emmet cut me off. "Later. There'll be plenty of time for questions. Now, listen up. I've got a story to tell you." In a voice filled with nostalgia, he began…

Chapter 53

Emmet's Story
Part I

The year was 1957, and 17-year-old Wayne Dunbar had worked as a busboy at The Goldstone Point Restaurant and Inn for less than a week when the tip came that federal agents were on the way. The Goldstone, a front for a well-known illegal gambling operation, was accustomed to such inconveniences, and young Wayne stood wide-eyed in the middle of the efficient chaos swiftly being executed around him. Blackjack dealers were securing their chips and flipping their tables upside down; then cocktail waitresses covered each flipped table with a tablecloth and dinnerware. Before his eyes, a gaudy gambling hall was quickly being transformed into an elegant dining room. A passing pit boss looked at

Wayne and decided his youthful muscles could be put to better use than just standing there gawking. "There's a dolly in the closet. Grab it and get those slot machines out of here!" he ordered.

Confused, Wayne stared at the man. "Dolly?" he mouthed.

"Yeah. It's in the closet. Hurry up!"

Wayne wasn't sure how a doll was going to help him move slot machines, but he went to the closet, nevertheless. Opening it, he saw a two-wheeled cart-like contraption with a metal lip on it. He didn't know if it was a "dolly" or not, but it looked like it could be used to move the slot machines. He grabbed it, wheeled it to the first of five slots, slid the lip under the machine's base, tipped it back onto the dolly's metal frame, and began ushering it out of the room. He knew he was supposed to hide the slot machines, and he knew that the adjacent cornfield was the usual hiding place for them, but as soon as he wheeled that first one through the back door, he stopped cold. It was spring. The corn wasn't tall enough to hide the slot machines.

Chapter 54

Emmet's Story

Part II

Wayne looked around. Where was he going to hide the slot machines? Then he heard the waves lapping on the shore and saw the dock a few short steps away. Wayne began to have other ideas… He started down the dock. The twelve-foot planks sagged a bit under the slot's weight, but the smooth boards made pushing relatively easy, nevertheless. Soon, he reached the end of the dock and peered into the lake's dark depths. With a quick shove and tip of the dolly, Wayne launched the first of the five slot machines into the lake.

He made four more trips. The first machine had been a nickel machine. The second two were quarters. The fourth was made for fifty-cent pieces. And the last was a dollar machine. Before Wayne wheeled the final slot down the dock, he found a softball sized rock on the shoreline and balanced it on top of the machine. When he got to the end of the dock, he took hold of the rock, brought it back, and with a crack splintered the glass face of the slot machine, spilling silver dollars onto the dock and into the water.

Chapter 55

Emmet's Story
Part III

With fumbling fingers, he took off his busser's jacket, shirt, and t-shirt. By knotting off the head and arm holes of the t-shirt, it made an effective make-shift bag. Kneeling on the dock, he scooped up two handfuls of coins and shoved them into his pockets and then tossed the rest of the coins into his t-shirt bag. After dumping the final slot machine into the lake, he put his dress shirt and jacket back on and did his best to scuff the remaining shards of glass off the dock.

By now, authoritative shouts were coming from in and around the casino. Without hesitation, he lugged the bag down the dock and hustled across the beach to where an old oak tree leaned out towards the water. Using his hands and a flat piece of wood that he'd picked up, he began digging a depression. When he'd dug a hole deep enough to cover the coin-filled shirt, he lowered it into the hole and covered it with sand. Wanting to leave no trace of evidence, he gave the piece of wood a heave towards the water. Curiously, there were two splashes — a large one, and then a moment later a much smaller one. Anxious to be done with the affair, he carefully began walking towards the oak tree while counting his steps. He'd gotten to seven when he was caught in the beam of a flashlight and heard, "Freeze!" Wayne froze.

"What do you think you're doing?" demanded the man behind the light.

"Just out for a walk," replied Wayne.

"Uh-huh. Dressed like that?"

Wayne looked down at his busboy uniform and could find nothing to say.

"I don't suppose you own a car?" the man growled. Wayne shook his head.

"I didn't think so. Well, here's the deal, kid. I don't know how you're mixed up in all this, but I think you're too young to be locked up. There's a train leaving in just over an hour. Be on it."

And Wayne, with two pockets full of silver dollars, was.

Chapter 56

Joey and I sat there wide-eyed, not knowing what to say.

Emmet continued, "I talked to my son in California yesterday. He watches my house and gets my mail for me when I'm gone. The other day he called and said a small package came for me. I told him to open it. It contained Wayne Dunbar's class ring."

I felt confused and betrayed. I'd grown to trust the man sitting next to me, and now I wasn't even sure if I knew his name. "Who are you, anyway?" I asked. "Emmet? Wayne? Or someone else?"

"You can call me whatever you like," he replied. "What's in a name? It's the person behind it that counts."

"If a name doesn't matter, then why do you have two?" I asked accusingly.

"I guess it's just convenient. When I'm treasure hunting, it saves me from having folks ask a bunch of personal questions that I don't feel like answering. I just tell them what they want to hear, and they go on their way. One story to them is as good as another."

'If you graduated in 1957," said Joey thoughtfully, "you must be –"

"That's right," said Emmet. "I'm over eighty years old. I try to eat right, and treasure hunting helps me stay in shape."

"You said you may have caused pain to our families. What's that about?" asked Joey.

"They don't even know you," I added.

"That may not be entirely true," said Emmet. "When I dumped the slot machines into the lake, nobody was aware of it. As a result, all of the casino employees were under suspicion for having taken them. In order to try to get someone to confess or rat someone else out, they pressed charges against all of the employees. Joey, your grandma was a cocktail waitress at The Goldstone, and Kyle, your grandpa was the pit boss. I'd read about the investigation in the papers, but I was too scared to come forward. Eventually, I moved overseas, life happened, and I tried to put it out of my mind."

It was Joey's turn again. "Why did you come back? For the silver dollars? Kyle checked you out. Wayne Dunbar is loaded. He's a multi-millionaire. A bag of silver dollars is hardly enough to move the needle for a guy like that. What gives?"

"You're right. I didn't and don't need the money. I just wanted to tie up the loose ends. I've been pounding around the world for the last twenty years or so chasing treasure tales, but this is the tale that I always come back to. Looking for treasure that someone else has lost or hidden is one thing, but finding a treasure that I'd hidden and then lost myself? That's something else entirely."

"So... did you?" I asked.

"Did I what?"

"Find the silver dollars?"

Emmet hesitated, looked around, motioned for us to come closer, and whispered, "I think so."

Chapter 57

In spite of our obvious impatience, Emmet wasn't in any hurry to tell us where the treasure was. Instead, he made himself a little more comfortable and continued, "When I got here, I didn't think I'd have any chance at finding my long-lost treasure. Everything had changed. The beach had narrowed, the oak tree was gone, buildings had been torn down and new ones built; but since I was here, I thought I might as well give it a shot and see if I could luck into them by randomly metal detecting up and down the beach." He looked at me, "I'd been here for over a week and was about to call it quits when you showed up."

"You stuck around because you thought I could help you? You've got to be kidding," I said, still not quite trusting his story.

"No. I stuck around because I thought I could help you."

"Oh."

There was a long pause while Emmet let that sink in. Finally, he continued, "This is a small town. It didn't take me long to learn a bit about the trouble you were in, and I sort of felt like I owed it to your grandpa. It may have been selfish on my part, but helping you out has eased my conscience some; and Joey, your showing up was a huge added bonus."

Chapter 58

I could see Joey's wheels spinning. Then, like a well-seasoned detective, he began, "Emmet, when I first got here, my grandma took me to the county museum. She said it would be educational. Anyway, I saw four old slot machines there that were said to have come from The Goldstone. Were they the ones you dumped in the lake?"

"Yes."

"Why were there only four? I thought you said that you dumped five in?" asked Joey.

"I did. A year or two after it was too late to help those who went to jail, some divers recovered the four machines that used silver coins; however, they left the nickel slot thinking that it wasn't worth the effort. By the time other folks started thinking that it'd be good to retrieve it for its historical significance, it couldn't be found – probably rusted to pieces."

"And your class ring," I said. "Why did you give it to me?

"I didn't need it. Your finding the location of that ring gave me all the information that I needed, so I thought you might like it. Besides, I was curious what you'd do with it. To tell you the truth, I didn't expect you to send it back to its millionaire owner."

I smiled and said, "Maybe I wouldn't have if I'd known what a jerk he was."

"So, Partner, are we good?" asked Emmet, holding out his hand.

"We're good," I said, and shook it.

"Hey!" said Joey. "What are we doing sitting around? Let's dig up some silver dollars!"

And we did.

Chapter 59

As I strolled into the courthouse the next morning with fifteen-hundred dollars in my pocket, I was feeling pretty good. Emmet had been right. Finding where he'd lost his ring had made locating where he'd hidden the silver dollars pretty easy. The beach had narrowed over the years, so where he had stashed the money had become overgrown with grass. He'd been searching the sandy area, and it had taken finding the ring to make him realize that he should be searching the grassy area that covered up what used to be a part of the beach years ago.

A few swings of the metal detector and some frantic digging soon revealed the remnants of Emmet's old t-shirt and too many silver dollars to count. As quickly and inconspicuously as possible, we transferred them to a five-gallon bucket and hauled them to Emmet's van. Once secured under a blanket in his backseat, Emmet whispered to us, "I'll meet you here tomorrow at the usual time with your share."

And he drove away.

Chapter 60

It had been tough seeing Emmet drive away with all that treasure, but true-to-his word, he met us at the beach the next morning and gave us cash for our share of the coins. In total, there had been 1,432 of them. At an average of $30 per coin, each of our shares came out neatly to $14,320.

At first, Joey wouldn't accept any of the money, saying that he was only in it for the fun and excitement, but we convinced him that since he helped find it, he should have a share as well.

Handing us each a manilla envelope thick with cash, Emmet said, "I'm not much of one for good-byes, but it's been a pleasure."

"Are you heading back to California?" I asked.

"Nope. No time for that. My son has a lead on

some Incan treasure, so I'm on my way to meet him in Ecuador. Take care, and keep digging!"

And he was gone.

I knew I'd miss Emmet, but the prospect of paying off my fine and having the rest of the summer to spend the remaining $12,820 sure helped relieve any pain caused by his departure. Finding that money was the best thing ever – until it wasn't.

Chapter 61

The line at the Clerk of Court's window was just as long as it was the first time I was there, and like the first time, when I finally reached the front of it, the same kind lady was waiting there to help me.

"What can I do for you today?" she asked.

"I've come to pay off my debt to society," I said, sounding a little brash.

She raised an eyebrow. "Your name, please?"

"Kyle Kennedy."

After a moment on her keyboard, she said, "That will be $1500. How would you like to pay?"

"Cash," I said, casually tossing my wad of hundred-dollar bills onto the counter in front of her.

"I see. Just a moment, please." She held a bill up

to the light and frowned. Then she held up another and another until she had looked at all fifteen. Picking up a phone, she spoke a few indecipherable words, turned to me, and said, "I'm sorry for the inconvenience, but there is someone who would like to visit with you before I can accept your payment."

Seemingly out of nowhere, two police officers had materialized, one on each side of me. One of them said, "Come with us, please."

And I did.

Chapter 62

The officers led me to a room with a sign above its door that read: SECURITY. The only other courthouse room that I'd been in was Judge Matheson's chambers, and by comparison, this one was extremely sparse: one table, four folding chairs. That was it.

"Have a seat," said one of the officers, as both of them sat down.

"You might as well make yourself comfortable," said the other.

I sat on one of the remaining chairs. It was cold and hard, much like everything else in the room, including the officers.

"My name is Officer Monroe," said the first officer. "And you remember Officer Davidson."

Now that I had a chance to get a better look at him, I did recognize Officer Davidson as the young policeman that came to see me at school nearly a month ago.

"We meet again," he said. "You've been busy."

I could feel my face turn bright red, unsure of what he was getting at. "Hi," I said weakly.

"You probably remember your Miranda rights," he said, "but just to be on the safe side, we better go over them again: You have the right to remain silent. Anything you say can and will be used against you in the court of law. You have the right to an attorney. If you cannot afford an attorney, one will be appointed for you. Do you understand your rights as I've read them to you?"

"Yes. Am I under arrest?"

"No, not yet, but we'd like to ask you a few questions. Is that okay with you?"

I didn't know what to say. The "not yet" concerned me, so I just said, "I don't know."

"We need a definitive answer," said Officer Monroe. "Will you answer some questions or not?"

I was scared. I didn't know what I could have done wrong. I wished my parents were there. "Can I remain silent until I call my parents?"

The officers exchanged looks.

"Sure," said Officer Monroe, "but in the meantime, we'll need to place you under arrest for attempting to pass counterfeit money. Please stand and lean with your hands against the wall."

Chapter 63

Even as I sat in the back of the squad car, it still didn't seem real. Emmet had double-crossed us! How could I have been taken in so easily? Suddenly, it all made sense: the secrecy, the payments in cash, and his sudden departure. He got the treasure, and we were left holding the bag. Even if we gave back all the fake money and told everyone the truth, who would believe us? Emmet, Wayne, or whoever he was, was gone, and there was no trace of evidence left to support our story. We were doomed.

Wait! I may be in a huge mess, but there wasn't any reason that Joey needed to be in one, too. Nobody knew that he played a part in this. Nobody knew that he, like me, was sitting on a pile of counterfeit money – at least, not yet. How could I let him know that the money was fake before he tried to spend it? Or had he spent some of it already?

Chapter 64

The odor in the back of the squad car was a noxious blend of boys' locker room and stale vomit. The handcuffs were chafing my wrists, and my arms, pinned between my back and the seat, were beginning to lose feeling. Officers Monroe and Davidson didn't seem like they'd be particularly sympathetic to my plight, but I thought a little complaining might be worth a shot.

"Officer Davidson?" I asked. "Do you think that maybe we could stop and let me stretch and get resituated? I'm losing circulation in my arms and can't feel my hands."

Neither officer said a word, but the car did slow down and come to a stop. It was not because of my request, however. We had come to a railroad crossing, and a train carrying car after car of grain was slowly slithering its way across the highway. In a flash, I could see the means of my escape – if only the train was long enough, and if only I could get out of the squad car.

Chapter 65

The train continued to slowly chug along. Time was running out. It was now or never.

"Since we're stopped anyway," I pleaded, "can I just get out and stretch for a minute?"

No response.

"Both my hands are numb."

Still no response.

"They feel like they're turning blue."

Nothing.

"They'll probably need to be amputated."

That got them. Officer Davidson got out and opened my door. "Hurry up," he growled. "This train only *looks* like it's going to take all day."

I got out, stretched, and said, "Do you mind maybe cuffing my hands in front of me? It's awfully uncomfortable when they're behind my back."

He gave me a long look and then slowly relented. Stepping behind me, he released one of the cuffs. Then, like being shot from a cannon, I exploded towards the train, matched its speed, darted between two cars, hurdled the coupling, and was free – at least for the time being.

Chapter 66

Three minutes and a phone call later, when the last train car had cleared the intersection, Davidson and Monroe found me standing on the opposite side of the tracks, patiently waiting for them. I'd accomplished my mission of texting a warning to Joey, so I saw little point in my running any further. Where would I go? What would I do when I got there? I figured my best option was to just throw myself on the mercy of the court, face the consequences, and move on. First, though, I would need to face the officers from whom I'd just escaped.

"Lie down on the ground! Put your hands behind your head!" yelled Officer Davidson. He was NOT amused by my brief escape from custody, and I guess I couldn't blame him. I had kind of taken advantage of his kindness. To his credit, though, even while visibly irritated, he remained professional as he cuffed me and bustled me back to the car. The remaining ride to the police station, however, was very quiet – and without any stops to stretch.

Chapter 67

When we got to the police station, I was brought to a small conference room where my parents were waiting for me. I had seldom seen my mother really upset with someone other than myself, but one look at her son in cuffs was enough to set her off. With red face and dagger eyes, she pointed to the handcuffs and fumed, "Really, officer? Are those *really* necessary?"

"He tried to escape, Ma'am," said Officer Davidson.

My father, wanting to avoid conflict, said diplomatically, "I appreciate your concern, Officer Davidson, but unless you feel that he is a physical threat..." And then I saw the corners of his mouth begin to twitch. What was going on? I couldn't believe it! He was trying not to laugh! What he found so humorous about the situation was beyond me, but then again, perhaps he and I were more alike than I realized. Maybe he, like me, didn't need a reason to find something funny. In any event, I dared not make eye contact with him for fear of bursting into laughter myself.

Officer Davidson looked appraisingly at me and said, "What do you think, Kyle? Done running?"

"Yes, sir."

With that, Officer Davidson took my handcuffs off and said, "Now that that's settled, have a seat, and let's get down to business."

Suddenly, there was a loud commotion in the hall, and a familiar young voice was shouting, "Kyle Kennedy! Where's Kyle Kennedy? He's innocent! Where's Kyle Kennedy?" Officer Davidson ran out the door. *Business*, it seemed, would have to wait.

Chapter 68

With Officer Davidson out of the room, my dad took the opportunity to quickly ask, "What's this we hear about you trying to spend counterfeit money? How in the world does that happen?"

"I don't know," I said. "It's a long story."

"In that case, you better hurry up and get started," said my mom. "Officer Davidson will be back any minute now."

I tried to fill them in as quickly as possible and was almost through when the door opened, and Officers Davidson and Monroe escorted a very excited Joey into the room.

"Hello, Kyle!" he exclaimed. "It's great to see you again! Are these your parents?"

My father stood and shook hands with Joey.

"Yes, I'm Ken and this is my wife, Laura. You must be Joey."

"That's right. I heard these guys were concerned about Kyle trying to spend some counterfeit money. Can you believe that? So I came on down to clear things up." He threw some of the bills that Emmet had given us onto the table. "I did some searching on the internet. These aren't counterfeit, they're just *old*!"

"Our apologies, Kyle – Mr. and Mrs. Kennedy," said Officer Monroe. "Our people have confirmed Joey's, uh… *research*. The bills aren't counterfeit. They're just so old that they raised suspicions when Kyle tried to use them to pay off his fine at the courthouse this morning."

"Then I'm free to go? And I can have my money back?" I asked.

Officer Monroe hesitated. "Well… yes, and no. You're free to go, but you'll both have to leave the money with us – and if you have any more, at home or elsewhere, you'll need to turn that in to the authorities as well. You see, it may not be counterfeit, but it *is* stolen. We ran the serial numbers, and they're tied to a 1934 bank robbery. I don't know how you came across those bills, but you'll need to forfeit them to the authorities."

Chapter 69

Emmet had been right. Finding treasure *was* a lot easier than keeping it. As soon as everything was straightened out and we were allowed to leave the station, Joey and I collected all of the remaining bills and went back to the police station where they would be turned over to the FBI. It was hard to see all that money slip through our fingers, but it was even harder to think that Emmet, who we thought was our friend, knew it was stolen and used it to get the silver coins free and clear.

As we were walking back to my place for lunch (It had been a LONG morning, and we were both starving.), Joey must have been thinking about Emmet as well, because he said, "Do you think Emmet knew the money was stolen?"

I thought about it a little more. As much as I wanted to believe that he knew nothing about it, I just couldn't convince myself that he didn't know, at the very least, that we'd run into trouble trying to spend those old bills. He could tell us all about every old coin that we found. Why wouldn't he also know about old paper money? "I don't know, Joey. I hope not."

We both walked in silence, each deep in our own thoughts. Finally, Joey said, "You know what we should do, don't you?"

"No," I answered. "What?"

"We should make sure Emmet knows that those bills are stolen, just in case he *doesn't* know.

"How are we going to do that? He's somewhere in South America for all we know. And it's not like he gave us his cell phone number or anything – if he's even got one."

"I know. But it wouldn't hurt to at least send him a letter."

"Snail-mail to the rescue?"

"It's worth a shot."

So as soon as we got back to my place, we wrote a letter to Wayne Dunbar.

Chapter 70

Now that I didn't have the stolen bank money, I still needed to come up with nearly three hundred dollars if I was going to pay my debt to society by Friday – now only a few days away. Fortunately, my grandma and grandpa, who lived on a farm just outside of town, needed their barn painted; and for a hundred dollars a day, it looked like I might be able to swing it – and if I couldn't, my parents, who had become uncharacteristically understanding as of late, said that they would help me out if I still needed more time.

When I got to my grandparents' place early Tuesday morning, Joey's bike was already leaning against the old walnut tree in the front yard, and the smell of bacon, eggs, and my grandma's famous

Danish crepe pancakes was wafting out of an open kitchen window. There was also a mingling of smells that I couldn't quite discern but were nevertheless equally enticing. My stomach growled. Breakfasts at my grandparents' farm were the best breakfasts ever! They almost made up for all the work that I'd be doing for the next few days.

Joey had volunteered to help me, and for that, I was grateful. Not only did many hands make light work, but his enthusiasm was infectious. Why he had chosen me to help out that summer, I didn't know, but I was sure glad he had. I'd found a good friend – or rather, a good friend had found me.

Chapter 71

When I walked into my grandma's kitchen, Joey was wallowing in culinary bliss. Bacon, eggs, pancakes, sausage, French toast, and creme puffs adorned his ginormous platter of a plate; and to wash it all down was strong black coffee, ice cold milk, and freshly squeezed orange juice. Even for my grandma, it was an extraordinary spread of gastronomical delights.

"Kyle!" Joey yelled as I walked in. "What were you thinking! I can't believe you had us digging in the sand every morning when we could have been sitting here gluttoning out on all of this glorious food. This is spectacular!"

My grandma beamed. "Oh, Joey, I know your grandma, and I'm sure she hasn't let you starve. But thank you all the same. It's good to have a couple of hungry young mouths to feed."

"As opposed to a hungry *old* mouth?" joked my grandpa.

"Exactly. It's so good to feed people who *appreciate* my food."

My grandpa laughed. "Joey, pass me some more of those cream puffs, please. It seems I need to show a little more appreciation."

Chapter 72

After we had all eaten as much as we could hold, Grandpa slid his chair back and said, "Gentlemen, it sounds like the two of you have had quite the interesting adventure. So how was old Wayne (or should I say Emmet) anyway? Did he tell you where the gold was?"

Joey and I exchanged confused looks.

Grandpa, seeing our confusion, mused, "Or maybe he doesn't know..."

Almost simultaneously, Joey and I blurted out, "Know what?"

"That he buried the silver dollars in the sand but dumped over a quarter million dollars in gold into the lake."

"What are you talking about?" I blurted.

Grandpa, enjoying the spotlight, just sat there and grinned.

"Mr. Kennedy," said Joey, trying to contain his excitement, "it sounds to me like you've been part of an adventure even more exciting than ours. Will you tell us about it?"

No response.

"Please?" he added.

Still no response.

"Aw," I said, giving Joey a knowing smile, "Grandpa is just messing with us. He doesn't know anything about any gold."

"Don't you be using any of that reverse psychology on me," blustered Grandpa. "I do know about gold. Lots of it – and that's not all I know. But for your own good, before I tell you anything, you need to promise me that you'll keep my story a secret. If someone knew you were looking for it, it could be dangerous. Gold can change people. So do you promise?"

We promised.

Chapter 73

Grandpa's Story
Part I

The year was 1957, and I, 25-year-old Kip Kennedy, had been working at The Goldstone Point Restaurant and Inn for a little over a year when the tip came that federal agents were on the way.

The Goldstone, as you know, was a front for a well-known illegal gambling operation. We had been raided several times in the past without incident, and at first, this raid seemed like it would be no different than the others. We were a well-run machine: Blackjack dealers secured their chips and flipped their tables upside down; the cocktail waitresses tossed tablecloths over the flipped tables and added silverware; and I put Wayne, a sturdy-looking busboy, in charge of removing the slot machines.

Wayne hadn't worked there very long, and we didn't really know a lot about him since he wasn't from around here, but he seemed like a good enough guy: friendly, hard-working, eager to please. So it didn't come as a surprise to me when he jumped right in when I asked him to grab a dolly and haul out the slots. In hindsight, I guess I should have known better.

Chapter 74

Grandpa's Story
Part II

Almost everything was ready. From all outward appearances, The Goldstone now looked like just a regular old restaurant and inn. The kitchen staff had even brought out some steaks and were serving them to some folks that just moments earlier had been rolling dice and playing cards. All that was left for me to do was stow away the night's take. By the heft of the money bag that held the house profits, I could tell that it had been a productive night. Several high rollers had flown into our town's little airport from Chicago, and they evidently had not had very good luck.

There was a walk-in safe located behind a secret panel in an office closet. I had memorized the combination and had deposited money in there more times than I could count. Maybe it was nerves. Maybe there was something wrong with the dial or tumblers. I don't know. What I do know is that no matter how hard I tried, that night, with the feds just minutes away, the safe just wouldn't open.

Chapter 75

Grandpa's Story
Part III

Panic began to set in. If I couldn't get the money into the safe, then I'd need to find a place to hide it. Wildly, I scanned the office. The desk was too obvious. The file cabinets would be ransacked. I could hear vehicles entering the parking lot… doors were slamming… footsteps… I froze. The money bag slipped from my fingers and landed on the wooden floor with a thud. Looking down, I could see that a couple bundles of tightly wrapped bills had escaped onto the floor. As they laid there, they seemed to be taunting me, encouraging me.

Greed is many terrible things: a devourer of dreams, a corrupter of souls, and a destroyer of families; but it can also be the inspiration for action. Quickly, I stuffed the rogue bills back into the bag, cinched the drawstring tight, took three quick steps towards an open window, and without hesitation, dropped the money bag between the outside wall and some tall ornamental shrubs. Mission accomplished. Or at least, so I thought.

Chapter 76

Grandpa's Story

Part IV

When I came back to The Goldstone early the next morning to retrieve my loot, it wasn't there. In its place, however, was a note that said: Be at Jo's Diner at 8:00.

Even in the fifties, Jo's was a bustling place. Every morning the tables were full, and the counter was crowded. Word of the previous night's escapades must have traveled fast, because when I walked in, I was welcomed by a round of applause, cheers, and several catcalls: "You sure showed them!" "Did you have special guests for dinner last night?" "I hope you showed our out-of-town guests a good time!"

Fortunately, I didn't have to be the source of their entertainment for too long, since from the far end of the room

I could see a hand high in the air emphatically waving to me. And Joey, the owner of that hand was your Grandma Margorie.

Chapter 77

Grandpa's Story
Part V

I jockeyed my way across the room and slid into a chair across from Margorie. She and I had become pretty good friends while working at The Goldstone, but at that moment, she wasn't one of my favorite people. I glowered at her and mumbled under my breath, "I thought you were my friend. Friends don't steal from friends."

She just laughed and said, "Look who's talking about stealing!"

I told her that I only pilfered a little from the Esposito brothers, the owners of The Goldstone, and that they'd never miss it. With the feds sniffing around, I figured they had bigger things to worry about than one night's receipts.

After a little haggling, Margorie and I said we'd split the money fifty-fifty. She had seen me dump it into the bushes and said that she deserved half of it for keeping the feds from finding it. I'm not sure that they would have, but possession is nine-tenths of the law, and she was the one who had possession. Or should I say HAD possession? You see, she didn't want the money traced back to her or me, so she gave it to her best friend for safekeeping, who just happened to be my girlfriend and future wife: Kyle's Grandma Barb.

Chapter 78

Grandpa's Story
Part VI

It turned out that it was a good thing that neither Joey's grandma nor I had kept possession of the money, because as we left the restaurant, we were both taken into custody by the authorities. Even though we'd pulled the wool over the Fed's eyes the night before, it soon became apparent that the Esposito brothers used the raid as an opportunity to clean house and wash their hands of the entire operation. They pressed charges against nearly all of The Goldstone employees, claiming that we had taken advantage of them and were running the illegal gambling hall without their knowledge.

Strangely enough, the Espositos never did seem to realize

that the night's receipts had gone missing. What they did notice, however, was that their five slot machines were gone, one of which was a high roller nickel machine converted to take five-dollar gold pieces – which just happened to be the same machine that Wayne dumped into the lake, and which just happens to be the same machine that could still be lying there today with over 500 five-dollar gold pieces still in its belly.

Chapter 79

Grandpa's Story
Part VII

The Espositos told us they'd make a deal with us, that they'd drop the charges for anyone who told them where the slots were. Unfortunately, as we've come to find out, the only person that knew where those slots were had taken a late-night train ride out of town. As a result, Margorie and I spent some time in prison. Nearly two years.

Fortunately, Barb was a trustworthy friend and loyal girlfriend. She could have run off with the money that had been left in her care and found somebody else; but instead, she invested it. According to Barb, there had been fifteen thousand in that bag of receipts, and by the time Margorie and I got out of prison, she had turned the original fifteen thousand into nearly forty – enough for her and I to get married and buy this farm. Margorie, on the other hand, used her share to go to college, get married, and eventually buy her lake house. In the end, I'd say things turned out pretty well.

Chapter 80

Grandpa's story had thrown Joey and me into stunned silence. Grandpa, appearing quite pleased with himself, grinned, began to get up, and announced, "There's work to be done! We better get at it. That barn isn't going to paint itself."

"No!" Joey and I yelled in unison.

"You have to tell us the rest of the story. You can't just leave us hanging!" I pleaded.

Grandpa settled himself back into his chair. "Well, what do you want to know?"

"Everything!"

"Like what?"

"Like did you ever try to find the slot with the gold in it?"

"No, I never looked for it. When they found the

other four slots, and left the "nickel" machine, I thought about it, but the farm kept me busy. Other folks who had worked at The Goldstone probably suspected the same thing that I had, so maybe one of them found it. I don't know. Good enough for them if they did. What I do know is that your dad never found it."

"What? Dad looked for it?"

"Sure. He and that friend of his spent hours swimming and snorkeling off that beach. They never found a trace of the gold, but they had a lot of fun trying. I often suspected that their 'treasure hunting' was just an excuse to get out of work and goof off."

I laughed at the thought. "Dad was a goof-off?"

"Of course he was. Look at me. Look at you. Apples don't fall far from the tree, you know. We were all goof-offs when we were kids – but then we grew up."

Chapter 81

When Grandpa said that my dad and he had eventually outgrown being goof-offs, he didn't need to elaborate. I knew I was a goof-off, he knew I was a goof-off, and we both knew that I didn't have to keep *being* a goof-off. He had changed, my dad had changed, and I could change. In fact, over the last few weeks, I think in some ways I sort of already had.

Emmet had said he'd stayed in order to help me. Is this what he meant? Or did he just use me to help him find the silver?

"Grandpa?" I asked, "Do you think Emmet set us up with the stolen money?"

"I don't know, Kyle. He hadn't been at The Goldstone very long when it got raided, so I didn't get to know him very well. It doesn't sound like he needed the money, but when it comes to treasure, people can do some pretty bizarre things."

"Is that why it might be dangerous for Kyle and me to look for the missing slot machine – because there's other people who know about it and are also looking for it?" asked Joey.

"Uh-huh. That's right. When the first four machines were found, I'm sure other former Goldstone employees like me were able to guess what was in the fifth one, and the Esposito brothers probably caught wind of it themselves. Of course, all those folks would either be old like me now or dead, but it is quite possible that some of them passed on the story to friends and family just like I've passed it on to you and your dad. It's also quite possible that some of those folks would be very interested if they knew someone was looking for it – or found it."

Chapter 82

Surprisingly, the three days it took to paint the barn turned out to be a welcome respite. Looking for treasure was exciting, but there was something to be said for the predictability of steady work, steady pay, and a steady stream of food.

My grandparents were sort of old school when it came to a meal schedule, and they were firm believers in eating early and often: breakfast at 6:00, lunch at 9:00, dinner at noon, coffee at 3:00, and supper at 6:00. That was a meal plan a teenager like me could really get behind.

Not only was the food excellent, but the actual painting had been kind of fun, too. Joey would sit in the tractor and run the loader bucket up and down while I stood in the bucket and ran the paint sprayer. When one area was covered, he'd move me on to the next. Our technique was so effective that we were done by Thursday morning and on our way to the courthouse by Thursday afternoon to pay off my debt. Joey had agreed to go along with me as moral support, but as it turned out, I didn't really need him since this time paying my fine went off without a hitch.

The funny thing was, as happy as I was to have gotten out from under the black cloud of debt that had been hanging over my head since the beginning of summer, I surprisingly felt a little sad, as well. For some reason that I couldn't quite explain, not having that debt left me feeling kind of empty. It had been the catalyst to one of my best summers ever, and then it was gone.

Chapter 83

Leaving the courthouse, I glanced over at Joey. "Thanks for coming with me."

"No problem. Any time."

"Well, I hope there won't be another time, but if there is, you'll be the first to know."

After a pause, Joey said, "You could let your parents be the first to know, you know. They seem really nice."

"What?" I asked, not sure that I heard him correctly.

"Your parents. They seem really nice."

"Why do you say that?"

"Let's see... Why are your parents nice?" he began. "For starters, perhaps we should look at how they treat that lousy, good for nothing, trouble-making son of theirs – who, by the way, happens to be one of the best pitchers that I've ever seen even though he doesn't even have enough ambition to even play on a team." Joey was really beginning to enjoy himself. "And in spite of all that, they continue to be there for him in his many times of need – whether the misguided miscreant appreciates it or not." Smiling, he gave me a shoulder-shove. "Am I right?"

I couldn't help but smile. He shoved me again. "Am I right?"

I guess sometimes a person needs to see what they have through the eyes of another in order to appreciate it. My parents certainly weren't perfect, but then again, neither was I. Who knows, maybe they were just trying to do the best they could with what they had where they were – making it up as they muddled along, just like everybody else. "Yeah. Sure. Everything considered, I guess you're right. But what made you think you needed to tell me that?"

"Because I wasn't sure you fully appreciated how good you've got it."

"How good *I* have it? What about you? Fancy boat at your disposal. Pitching varsity ball. No parents around to nag you." I laughed and gave Joey a shove, but he wasn't laughing. "What's wrong?"

"You know why I'm at the lake this summer?"

"To play ball."

"That's only part of it. The truth is that I'm an inconvenience to my parents."

"Whatever. *Every* kid is an inconvenience to their parents. That's nothing special."

Joey looked like he was about to bawl. "How many parents send their kid to camp or to a relative every single summer to keep them out of their hair?"

"I don't know. Probably quite a few, actually."

"Maybe. But how many also pay their kid not to be a bother to them?"

"What? They pay you? How much?"

"Three thousand a month for good behavior. If I mess up and cause them any inconvenience, they deduct a thousand dollars from my pay for each offense."

"You've got to be kidding. That can't be true," I said incredulously.

"Nope. I'm not kidding. When I was just a kid, I overheard them yukking it up with another couple about how having a kid wasn't going to slow them down. They said, and I quote, 'We can always make more money, but we can't make more time; so Joey will always get plenty of our money, and we'll get to keep our time for ourselves. Everyone will be happy.'"

For a few long moments I was speechless. When I was finally able to blurt something out, all I could say was, "Wow. Just wow. I'm sorry."

"I know a lot of kids have it worse than I do, but it still stinks."

I asked, "So is that why you're such a 'Good Samaritan' – helping to sift day after day without wanting anything for it, helping to find a pile of silver and not wanting any of it, and then helping to paint an entire barn for no more than some good eats?"

"Yeah. I really don't need any money, but I do need to feel like I'm wanted – that I belong somewhere. My parents don't care where I am as long as I'm not bothering them, but you and Emmet would have cared if I hadn't shown up to sift or paint or whatever. It's good to know that someone is counting on you. I think that's why I've always liked baseball – especially pitching. Lots of people counting on you."

"So now what?" I asked.

He shrugged and gave me a little grin. "I say we go to your house, raid the kitchen, and spend some time celebrating your paying off your debt to society. Maybe toss the ball around a little. I've got a game tonight, and I'd like to loosen my arm up a bit. Sound good?"

"Yup. Sounds good."

Chapter 84

When we opened the door to the kitchen, we were greeted by the smell of freshly baked cookies.

"Yes!" exclaimed Joey. "I knew coming here was a great idea."

"Not so fast," I warned, "We're entering *The Danger Zone.*" With my folks at work, there was only one explanation for the source of those cookies: The Troll.

"What? What are you talking about? I thought we were talking about cookies. What's so dangerous about cookies?"

"You'll see."

"Hello, Kyle. Who's your friend?" cooed a deceptively innocent voice, and from out of the pantry closet waddled The Troll.

"This is Joey. Can we have some cookies?" I began reaching for what looked like a warm and gooey chocolate chip cookie. "OUCH!" A spatula had mysteriously materialized out of nowhere and smacked my hand.

The Troll shook her mangy head. "Kyle, Kyle, Kyle…" she chided, "you should know better than that. These cookies aren't for you. They're for the summer Bible school kids. Of course, I need to sample them first." With that, she opened her giant maw, tossed down a cookie, smacked her lips, and said, "Yep. They'll do just fine, but they'd be even better with a cold glass of milk." She turned and began a slow and deliberate waddle towards the refrigerator. "By the way, you've got mail."

"What?"

"You know. Mail. A letter. It's from the school and looks official. I left it on the table."

Yep. There on the table lay a letter. "It's been opened."

"Of course it's been opened. How could I read it if I didn't open it?"

"It's against the law to open other people's mail, you know."

"Sue me."

I sighed, "So what did it say?"

"It says that the July school board meeting is Monday night, and they'd like you to be there. They're going to decide if you should be permanently expelled or not."

For the past month, I'd tried not to think about the possibility of my being permanently kicked out of school, but in just three more days, it looked like I was going to have to face the reality of that possibility whether I wanted to or not.

The sight and smell of the cookies was overpowering. Her back was turned. Should we risk it? The temptation was great, but the memory of the spatula smack still lingered. No longer able to stand it, Joey broke. "What do we need to do to get a cookie?" he pleaded.

With catlike quickness, The Troll pounced on his show of weakness. "Oh, I don't know. Perhaps if you bag and box the rest of these cookies and put them in my car, I'd be able to spare a couple."

An hour and several trips to The Troll's car later, Joey and I sat on the steps of our front porch, each with exactly two cookies and a cold glass of milk. Well played, Troll. Well played.

Later that night, I got a text from Joey: Meet me

at the beach in the morning. Usual time. I've got an idea.

Chapter 85

When I got to the beach, the sun was just peeking over the horizon, a slight breeze periodically dappled the lake's otherwise still surface, and a sleek blue and white ski boat sat tied to the dock, looking restless as it gently tugged at its mooring lines. Sitting in the captain's chair was Joey, with a huge grin on his face and a dive mask on his head.

"What's up?" I asked as I felt the wooden planks spring against my feet as I made my way down the dock.

"It's gold-finding time!" announced Joey, who seemed to be very pleased with himself.

"SHHHH. Quiet!" I couldn't help but look around to see who may have heard. Working with Emmet had made me a bit paranoid. "What do you mean, 'It's gold-finding time?'"

In a slightly quieter voice he said, "I *mean* I know how we can find that last slot machine."

"You win. How?"

"I'll show you."

He unfastened the line near the bow of the boat but left the line near the stern attached. Then he put the engine in gear. Slowly, the boat's bow swung out until the entire boat was perpendicular to the dock, continuously tugging against the still-attached line.

I don't think I had ever seen Joey more excited. *Why,* I wasn't sure. Then, with an even bigger grin (if that was possible), he said, "Watch this!" He hit the throttle. I could feel the dock shudder as it fought the pull of the motor. Joey pointed behind the boat. "Look!" Huge plumes of sand and sediment were billowing out from the prop wash. It was an impressive sight, but I wasn't sure at first of the significance. Then I noticed Joey's goggles again, and it hit me: We were going to use the force of the boat's motor to uncover the lost slot!

Chapter 86

For the next couple of hours, we carried out Joey's plan. We took turns being in and out of the boat. The one in the boat was in charge of slowly fanning the motor back and forth in order to blow a huge hole in the sand. The one in the water (making very sure that the boat's motor was in neutral so as not to get sliced by the spinning prop) would periodically dive behind the boat and eyeball any treasure too heavy to be blown out of the hole.

It was a good plan. We were finding more items faster than we'd ever found by sifting. Taking a break, Joey and I surveyed our newfound pile of plunder lying on the bottom of the boat: miscellaneous pieces of brass, old swim tags and buckles, coins of all dates and denominations, several silver rings, and even a couple of gold ones. If we hadn't been hunting for bigger game, we'd have been extremely happy with our results.

"This is fun," I said, "but we're going to have to get pretty lucky just randomly blowing out holes like this."

"I wish we knew where the other four slots were found," lamented Joey wistfully.

Then we heard a familiar voice from behind us say, "Then you might want to try the next dock over."

Joey and I looked at each other, looked at our pile of treasure, and knew that we were busted. What we were doing was obvious. There was no hiding it. Though we didn't think we were really doing anything wrong, we still were more than a little embarrassed to have someone catch us at it after Emmet had taught us to be so careful. Slowly, we stood and turned around.

"Hi, Coach," I said.

"Yeah. Hi, Coach," added Joey.

"It looks like you're having pretty good luck," he said as he eyed our treasure, "but if I were you, I'd shut things down. If the authorities notice what you're doing, you may have some explaining to do."

"What do you mean?" I said defiantly. "We're not doing anything illegal." Then, with a little less confidence, I added, "Are we?"

"What do you think?" said Coach as he pointed to where we'd been searching. "You're intentionally tearing up the bottom of the lake and leaving it a mess. Don't you think there might be a law against that?"

The water had cleared, and I could easily see the series of holes that we'd blown cratering the bottom of the lake. Legal or illegal, I could see that what we were doing *was* wrong, and at that moment I was pretty ashamed of myself. One of the first rules that Emmet had taught me was to leave things as good or better than I'd found them, and I'd broken it. "I don't know," I mumbled.

"And you, Joey, I expected more from you. Your grandma lets you use her boat, and this is how you treat it? And more importantly, what do you suppose would happen if you accidentally put it in gear while Kyle was under the water back there? Or if you were diving and *he* put it in gear?"

Joey murmured, "I don't know," but I knew he really did know because his voice was quavering as he said it.

"Well, the two of you sure don't know much," Coach concluded.

"Sorry, Coach," I said.

"Yeah, sorry, Coach," added Joey.

Coach just stood there. Gradually, his gaze shifted from us to all of the blown-out holes, and then it drifted to the next dock over. Then a funny thing happened. His demeanor suddenly changed, and he said, "Kyle, your dad may not have ever mentioned it, but he and I spent many hours looking for that slot machine. Never did find it. Could never get down deep enough through all that sand." After a pause, he continued, "You boys should give this up, but if you don't, you better make sure you get here really early in the morning in order to avoid any conflicts – if you know what I mean. Good luck!" And he left.

Joey and I just sat with our mouths open.

"Wow," I said finally.

"Yeah. Wow," Joey added.

"I can't believe Coach was the friend that my dad searched for the slot with."

"And I can't believe that he was nice enough to tell us where to look! This is great! Let's get over there and find it!"

I could hardly believe my ears. Joey no longer seemed at all phased by Coach's speech. "Are you kidding? You heard what Coach said. What we're doing is not just stupid but maybe even illegal." I looked around nervously. "Besides, if Coach saw us, someone else might, too. Someone not quite so helpful – or nice."

"Come on, Kyle. Let's blast one more hole just to see. You know you want to. Especially now that we have a better idea of where to look."

I didn't know what to say. Until Coach pointed it out to us, I hadn't considered that there might be anything wrong with what we were doing. I'd gotten in enough trouble for one summer, and I didn't need to get in any more. On the other hand, I didn't want to let Joey down, and he was right. I *did* want to keep looking–maybe even more than he did. Not only would finding the gold be great, but finding the gold that my dad couldn't find would be amazing. I shrugged my shoulders. "Okay. But let's be extra careful. Deal?"

"Deal."

Chapter 87

Soon we found out that *saying* we'd be careful was one thing, and *being* careful was another. I untied the dock rope and shoved off. Joey put the boat in gear, began to swing it out away from the dock, and CLUNK! The motor quit, and the boat lurched to a stop. Both of us grabbed to hold on as we were tossed forward onto the dashboard. Fortunately, we weren't going very fast, so we were mostly just surprised and a little bruised. If we had been racing across the lake, though, it may have been a different story.

"What happened?" I asked.

"I don't know. I'll raise the motor. Maybe I hit something."

Joey turned off the motor and pushed the

button that should have raised it, but there was only a buzzing sound, and the motor didn't budge.

"It's like it's stuck," he said.

I went to the back of the boat and took a look. "Uh-oh… It *is* stuck. It appears that someone forgot to put a tie rope back in the boat. It's all wrapped around the prop."

"Hmmm…" said Joey, looking at me. "I wonder who that 'someone' was?"

"The same someone who's going to have to jump in and unwrap it, I guess."

I hopped over the side. Since the water was fairly shallow, I could stand on my tiptoes while I worked, so unwrapping the rope turned out to be not too huge of an ordeal; however, it did take some time, time that we didn't really have if we didn't want more people to notice what we were doing.

"Joey, maybe we should just call it a day and come back in the morning – for one last time. Okay?"

"Alright," he conceded. "How does 4:30 sound?"

"It sounds early, but I'll be too excited to sleep anyway."

"I know. How can we sleep knowing that a quarter million in gold coins is *right over there?*"

Chapter 88

"Today's the day that we get our pay!" announced Joey as I walked down the dock – the dock that Coach said could lead us to the missing slot machine.

"I hope so. I'm wondering, though, if our enthusiasm may have gotten a little bit ahead of a rather significant logistical consideration: How are we going to see under water when it's still almost dark out?"

"You use big words, you know that?"

"Yup. Now answer the question: How are we going to see under water when it's so dark?

"We don't. Since this is such a momentous (I can use big words, too.) occasion, we'll just relax and revel in the moment while we have a bit of breakfast and wait for the sun to finish coming up."

So in the predawn chill, we sat in Joey's grandma's boat and ate warm cinnamon rolls that had been carefully wrapped in aluminum foil and washed them down with cold milk from a well-worn Thermos, and we looked back on our summer and talked about how it was unlike any summer either of us had ever had before.

We talked about Emmet, and sifting, and whether or not he meant to cheat us by giving us the stolen money, and where he was now, and what he was doing. Did he find the treasure he was looking for? Would we find the treasure that *we* were looking for?

The dark turned to gray, and the gray turned to a subtle spectrum of pastel hues, painting the sky in delicate shades as the sun prepared to rise. Then in a vibrant burst of colors, dawn unfolded with a breathtaking sunrise, and at that moment, Joey and I realized that regardless of whether we found the missing slot or not, we'd already struck gold.

Chapter 89

Joey positioned the boat to blast the first hole. "How does this look?"

"Looks good to me."

He revved the motor and blasted away. When he was done, he shut off the motor and turned towards me. The huge grin that I'd noticed the first day we'd worked together was again plastered across his face.

"Rock-paper-scissors for who goes first?" I asked.

"No. You go ahead," offered Joey. "If it's there, I think you should be the one to first lay eyes on it."

"If you say so. Wish us luck!"

I took a deep breath, jumped in, and made my way to the back of the boat. Almost immediately, I saw something just to the side of the blasted-out hole. Still partially covered in sand and silt was what looked like a big old box with gaping rusted out holes in it. For a moment I was confused, but then I noticed the long handle with a knob on it, and I realized that what I was looking at was the long-lost slot machine!

Through the rusted-out holes, I could make out some of its inner workings as well as a pile of small gold discs. I grabbed a handful and pushed off towards the surface. As soon as I broke clear I yelled, "We've found it!" and gave the handful of gold pieces a toss. A small cascade of gold rained into the boat.

"Woo-hoo!" yelled Joey, and he plunged into the lake to join me.

With both of us working, it didn't take long before we had our mesh finds bag nearly half filled with coins. When it looked like we'd gotten all there was to get, Joey gave the signal for us to bring it up.

Hauling all that gold to the surface proved to be more of a struggle than we'd anticipated. Even with the two of us, swimming with the bag of gold was a formidable challenge. Lungs burning, legs and arms aching, we finally were able to break the surface. With one giant heave, we flopped the gold-filled bag over the side of the boat.

That's when we heard it. Someone was applauding: *Clap… Clap… Clap…*

Chapter 90

Out of breath, sputtering water, and physically spent, we crawled into the boat to find Coach comfortably seated in the captain's chair with the bag of gold on his knee and its tie string securely wrapped around his wrist. If possession is nine-tenths of the law, it was obvious to all of us that Coach was definitely now in possession of the gold. He'd played us like a fiddle, and it looked like we were going to pay for it.

"Well done, boys! Well done. You've been able to do what no one else has." Then a hard edge crept into his voice. "Now untie us and shove off. We're going for a little ride."

"Where are we going?" asked Joey.

He nodded towards the anchor lying on the

bottom of the boat and in a gruff voice growled, "The Cliff."

One of the reasons that our lake was so clear was that it was spring fed and deep. Very deep. And the deepest part of the lake was just to the west of a huge one-hundred-fifty-foot dropoff that was called The Cliff. If Coach dumped us there with an anchor tied to us, not only would we most certainly drown, but we would also most likely never be found. Nobody would ever know what had happened to us. We had been warned that treasure – especially gold – could do strange things to people, and it was apparent that that was definitely true for Coach.

Chapter 91

The ski boat skittered across the lake at over fifty miles an hour. We knew that at that rate, it wouldn't be long until we were at The Cliff and permanently swimming with the fishes. If we didn't do something soon, it would be too late to do anything at all. I frantically looked around for something, anything that would be helpful. Then my gaze fell on one of the tie ropes that I'd carelessly tossed onto the bottom of the boat next to where Joey was sitting.

My eyes got wide. Why hadn't I thought of it sooner? I looked at Joey and saw that he had followed my gaze to the rope, and from the fear on his face knew that he had read my mind and didn't like what he'd found there.

"No," he mouthed.

"We have to," I mouthed back.

Resigned to the inevitable, he gave a little nod. Then he nonchalantly tossed the tie rope over the side. We saw it flutter and bounce behind the boat maybe four or five times before our world exploded into a dazzling display of light, water, and sound. The combination of high speed and a rope-wrapped motor caused the boat to careen violently to starboard, flipping us out of the boat and cartwheeling us several feet across the surface of the lake until we landed with a splash.

I came up spitting and sputtering and began treading water. "Joey! Are you okay?" I yelled.

"Yeah! You?"

"I'm good. Where's Coach?"

Then we heard it: "Help!"

Somehow, perhaps because of where he was located in the boat, Coach hadn't been tossed as far as Joey and I had. In fact, he couldn't have been more than four or five yards from it. However, for some reason, he was struggling to get to it. "HELP!" he yelled again.

Then we saw why he was struggling. He still had a hold of the bag of gold. "Let go of the gold!" I yelled.

"No!"

His head was barely above water. Time was running out.

"We're on our way!" yelled Joey. "Drop it!"

"I won't!"

For a moment, his head briefly slipped below the surface but then popped back up.

"Drop the gold! Do it *now*!" I commanded.

I was getting closer. Close enough to see his eyes. Close enough to see that there was something in them, something that I couldn't understand. Something that I didn't want to understand.

I reached out my hand. He grabbed it. We both went down, struggling, flailing. We popped back up but almost immediately went back down. Surfacing again, I could see Joey was closer but not close enough. I tried to get a better hold on Coach, but it wasn't working. The gold was too heavy, too awkward. We were going down again. Fear swept over me. I screamed at Coach, "LET GO OF THE GOLD!"

"I *can't!*" he whispered – and let go of my hand.

Epilogue

"STRIKE ONE!"

It was good to be playing baseball again, and it was especially good to be on the pitcher's mound. It wasn't that I'd completely gotten over being anxious and nervous, because sometimes I still was, especially when the count was full; but after what I'd been through, I realized that baseball, win or lose, was only a game, and I just needed to appreciate the opportunity to play it.

"BALL."

They never did find Coach or the bag of gold. If it hadn't been for the remnants of the old slot machine and the handful of gold pieces that I'd tossed into the boat, it's possible that nobody would have believed that our treasure tale had happened at all.

"BALL."

As it was, the school board said that due to extenuating circumstances, I could attend school again in the fall and even play baseball for the remainder of the summer.

"STRIKE TWO!"

As for Joey, he had to go back home when it became known that he wasn't eligible to be on the team – and any game that he had played in had to be forfeited. His parents said that they may move here before long in order to be closer to his grandma, so maybe by next summer he and I will be on the same team.

"BALL."

I still wonder about Emmet. Where is he now? What is he doing? Did he get our letter? For better or worse, without him, this summer would have never happened.

"TIME!"

Heads turned as several patrol cars sped in and cordoned off the practice field adjacent to the diamond. Soon, the dull roar of a helicopter could be heard in the distance. Getting louder and louder, it was obviously getting closer by the second.

Finally, with a flourish of sight and sound, a pitch-black helicopter swept over the treetops and landed in the middle of the practice field.

When the blades came to rest, a barrel-chested giant of a man stepped out and strode on tree trunk legs towards the stands. A black tailored suit had replaced the red flannel shirt and cut-off jeans, but there was no mistaking the man with the intelligent soft blue eyes framed by a thick white beard and bushy eyebrows.

"PLAY BALL!"

Bottom of the seventh, two outs, bases loaded, full count... One pitch. That's all it would take. One pitch. My heart started to race. The old worries and anxieties began to creep in. Then I heard a familiar voice say, "Dig deep, Kyle. Dig deep."

And I did.

ABOUT THE AUTHOR

For over thirty years, Dan Willadsen has been an English teacher in the Midwest. He claims that every student that he has taught has been remarkable in their own unique way but acknowledges that he himself was probably not always the easiest student to have in class – as evidenced by the fact that many of his earliest writing efforts were lines and lines of "I will not talk in class. I will not talk in class. I will not talk in class…"

Willadsen grew up fishing and metal detecting at a resort town not far from his family's farm and still enjoys fishing and metal detecting today. He admits that he has never struck it rich, but perhaps that is just because he hasn't dug deep enough yet.